I Pinkie Promise

That our love will live long after our memories are forgotten

I0545336

A Novel by Saif Rebai

SABRESTORM
STORIES

Edited, designed and typeset by Sabrestorm Stories Ltd.

British Library Cataloguing in Publication Data
A catalogue record for this book is available from the British Library

Published by Sabrestorm Stories Ltd., The Olive Branch, Caen Hill, Devizes, Wiltshire SN10 1RB United Kingdom. Company number 11927154.

Website: www.sabrestormstories.com
Email: enquiries@sabrestormstories.co.uk

ISBN 978-1-913163-04-4

I Pinkie Promise is the debut novel from
Saif Rebai, BBC Arabic Presenter and
renowned YouTube Comedian.

I Pinkie Promise

One

I opened my eyes just seconds before the alarm on my phone reminded me that it was another day for me to go to work, decorate my face with a smile, put on a tie, and go do something I hate for eight hours. But we will get to that in a moment. I stared at the ceiling, and asked myself the three questions I ask myself every day: What am I doing with my life? What is my purpose in this world? Can I have ten more minutes of sleep? Every day, I looked for the answers but could only find one for the third question, no, I can't have ten more minutes of sleep! So, I shoved my head in the pillow one more time, kissing it goodbye, and pushed the covers away. If there is anything that makes my mornings tolerable and makes me some kind of a morning person is the breakfast I cook. I love taking my time to prepare something that I spoil myself with. I wish it were as exciting as I make it sound in my head, but it's nothing to be honest, just an omelet, some waffles with chocolate drizzled all over them, and a hot coffee that saves me every day from the cold waiting outside.

I'm not such a good friend with sleep. We barely meet for a couple of hours, and then we say our goodbyes even before the sun wakes the world up. So, I take my time getting ready, cooking whatever I feel like eating, and just enjoying the early morning sunrays that travel slowly through my window every day. I enjoy that so much that I lose track of time sometimes, and today was one of those times.

My phone rang and it was Steven from work. Oh, Steven, my dear friend, who to this day I can't believe I can call my friend. I can describe Steven by saying that this world is full of Stevens. He is the type of guy everyone wants to be like and to be friends with. The cool guy with the big smile on his face that helps him get around in life. He is very successful in the company we work at and plays with the top players there.

"Hey, Steven, morning."

"Yo, bro, up yet? I'm going to swing by your house if you want a ride. I'll be there in five minutes."

I said to myself, *five minutes - why is he coming this early?* Then I checked the time and, dear God, I freaked out from how late I was.

"You are a lifesaver, man. I lost track of time. I'm getting ready, see you in a bit."

"I've never seen someone wake up as early as you do and still be late for work, man. Be there in a minute, don't make me wait," Steven said, laughing.

I think I didn't quite lose track of time as much as I tried to make myself forget where I would be as soon as I left this place to head to the land of the dead, or as other people would call it, *work*, but I still need to put food on this table, so thank God Steven was going to give me a ride. I ran to my room, put on my work clothes, my coat, my sunglasses, grabbed my backpack, and started looking for my shoes that somehow decided to bail on me and disappear as they always did. I started to stress and pray that it wouldn't be one of those days that just starts off really bad and turns out to be even worse later. I stressed even more when I heard Steven pulling up.

"Hey, Steven, I'll be down in a second," I shouted from my window.

My apartment isn't that big. There aren't a million places they could be. I hate it when I know something is just under my nose and I can't see it. *Breathe, Zayn, breathe.* I looked under the bed, and whoop! There goes one shoe, and the other one was next to the door. God only knows how it got there. It was as if it moved on its own when I was asleep, I swear, or maybe someone moved it. *No, no, no, don't think about ghosts, you will be up all night. You just left it there, so shut up, okay. You barely sleep as it is and don't need another reason to stay up all night.* I closed the apartment door and ran towards the red Corvette

"Hey, Steve, sorry for being so late. I swear it's not my fault, it's these damn shoes."

"Dude, it's all right, don't worry about it, we still have time," said Steven, laughing at me trying to get myself together next to him. I saw it in his eyes that he was probably trying to come up with a joke to embarrass me.

I cut him off by saying, "So, how are you? How is everything? I didn't see you around the office for a while."

"Actually, life is good. Mary is moving in with me. Things are getting really serious with her, and I'm actually thinking that I'm not going to screw it up this time. As for work, I moved to the sixteenth floor. Katherine thought it time for me to step up my game, so yeah, I play in the elite league now."

"I'm really happy for you, dude. I hope you don't forget about me after they suck you into their five-star world."

I can see him rolling his eyes and without even looking at me, he punched me on the shoulder for the comment I made, so I finished laughing. "I didn't mean suck you in that way! I'm sure you're going to do great there. As for Mary, just lose contact with the other girls, please. I know that you attract women like flowers do to honeybees, and it's not your fault that you are irresistible to them, like you always say, but please, just listen to me and let that Casanova side of you die peacefully and focus on the gift that Mary is."

"You are mean, man! I know I'm irresistible, but I would never say it out loud like that," Steven laughed. "Okay, fine, I'll stop. Enough about me, what's going on with you? Is Janice still giving you a hard time? Should I talk to her?"

"No, Steven, I'm okay. I learned to live with her constant criticism of everything I do, so I guess I'll just keeping that anger inside until one day I snap and shove her head inside the copying machine that is my life."

Oh, the copying machine is actually my job. Right, you thought that I use it for my work. No, it is actually the whole package. I'm the guy who is always standing next to the machine waiting for people to give me a paper to copy, hand it back to them with a smile, and stand there in silence waiting for the next person to come up. I have Janice still criticize me because, somehow, she thinks that I either took too long doing that, or I'm not doing it right. Copying Machine Guy is not my dream job, but in this world, there is a big difference between dreams and reality. Dreams are the light that we always keep chasing so we don't get scared of the future and what it might hold for us, or to be more precise here, what the future might not hold for us. As for reality, it's that gloomy, gray cloud that covers the sun and makes what used to be a beautiful day turn into a black and white stage of sadness. It covers our light and lets us fall into constant fear of not growing to be the heroes we thought we would, with the fear of not being able to provide and put food on the table. I'm in that stage now, but hey, I think I can still dream from time to time, so I'm okay, I guess.

Steven laughed, "I wish I could be there to witness her unleash her wrath on some of the people there."

Steven is one of those people who, as soon as you look at him you know that he is a big deal somewhere. He always has this bright smile that he faces the world with, and I honestly envy that in him. No matter what he is going through, and I know for a fact that sometimes he is not that happy with a lot of things, but that never shows up on his face. He never lets his problems crawl onto this façade he builds, and I honestly wish I had that type of strength. I wish I had that gift, but hey, maybe I'm not as strong as he is for a reason.

We were almost there, and I looked at Steven scrolling around music stations on his fancy radio. I asked myself a question that probably no one can answer: how did it happen? How am I friends with someone like him? I mean, there is no chance that sixteenth-floor people would even look at copying machine guys like me. It's unheard of! People at the office are actually jealous of the friendship we have. Sadly for me, seeing me with Steven sometimes during lunch is the one thing some people remember me for in this company. Some of them call me 'Steven's Friend', because they don't even know or care to remember my name.

We became friends just when I started my famous position as the president of the copying machine department, and I remember it as if it were yesterday. It was my second day there, and as I was learning how to use the machine when a whole stack of documents got jammed inside it and it started to make a weird, loud noise that made everyone stop whatever they were doing and look at me. And that was my first introduction to our dearly, beloved Janice, who came and screamed and humiliated me like no one ever did. As she was about to unleash her two favorite words on me "You're fired!" Steven intervened. He used that charm he has that somehow works even on extra-terrestrial creatures like Janice, and, surprisingly, he calmed her down by saying, "He's new, Janice. Come on, cut him some slack. He'll get it sorted. Let me get you a coffee, black no sugar, the way you like it, right?"

He gave me a look that I'll never forget while he was talking to Janice and walking with her back to her office. A look of 'get yourself together and welcome to the real world'. I never forgot, and probably never will, how much that meant to me, even though, looking at it now, I wish he hadn't stopped her. I wish she had fired me. That would have been a gift. I strongly need the gift of unemployment that most people would be scared of, but if she had, maybe I wouldn't be as lost as I am today. Maybe not having a job would have helped me to find what I really want to be and do in this world, but I can't be all sad about it because that's what started my friendship with Steven.

We got to his parking spot and walked together to the elevator. And as the door opened all you could hear was, "Steven, good morning." "Steven, how are you today, sir? See you at lunch, Boss." And it was the funniest thing ever because I knew for a fact that those people didn't even like him that much, but his place in the company forced them to suck up to him like that. So, what I did was stand in the corner and watch the people trying their best to get his attention, proving the fact that it's in our human nature to seek approval from people who we see as superior to ourselves.

Why is that a thing? Why do we always treat people differently just because of their appearance, or their work, or where they are from? Why do we never look behind the curtains and evaluate what this pretty face and that expensive suit hides underneath it?

There is no point looking for an answer to these questions because I believe that it's the way our human brain is built, and there is no point in trying to understand it because it will always be like that. I left the crowd of cheerleaders surrounding Steven and exited the elevator on the third floor, right where all the useless people hide. I walked ahead and did what I do best and that is disappear into my own small world of pressing buttons and copying paper and do it with a smile on my face because a frown could actually get you fired here if Janice feels like it.

I found a way of making it a bit easier through almost every day. I would disappear and press these buttons and serve documents to people while my brain was surfing somewhere else.

It usually floated around here and there with no actual destination or purpose of what to think about. Sometimes it would be life decisions, and most of the time it would be silly stuff that had no use in my life except help me get through my days here. Today, it decided to take me to a place and time that I genuinely miss, a cold, rainy November day exactly twelve years ago.

My father passed away that year, and I was just a little kid who knew nothing of this world's misery and sadness. That was the first time I sipped from the bitter cup of loss that this life hides for all of us. I never was the same after that, even though God blessed us humans with the gift of what I call 'moving on no matter what.' I was broken, and it didn't matter how much love my mother tried to surround me with, I wasn't able to get fixed. All his life my father tried his best not to let me feel that I could lose something. You hear people say all the time that their dad is Superman, well mine actually was. He never let sadness find its way to the heart of his one and only son. He fought the smallest things that could upset a kid like me to the point where he argued with my mom because she was afraid that I would grow up to be a spoiled kid who would always rely on his father for everything. He never listened to her. If a toy of mine broke he would stop everything and fix it. If we ran out of my favorite ice cream he would run and get it for me, even in the middle of the night, and he would sneak it into my room and we would eat it together under the covers, afraid that my mom would find out and punish both of us. I was happy inside and outside my home. Even at school, in those hard times where kids decide that they won't like you and just bully you unstoppably, he was there. He used to read my tears when I got back home all muddy and messed up from what they did to me, and he knew no fear and kept on saying, "Oh, if they bully my boy, I will bully them and their parents, and their grandparents," and he would leave the house and make their lives a living hell.

He was there unconditionally, until one day, one sad, November day everything changed. It was raining, and I remember that because I had an assignment in class that I'll never forget. My art teacher told us to draw something imaginary, a scene or a place where we would rather be. I drew myself holding my father's hand and walking through a vast field of wheat. My imagination made me draw us surrounded with scary monsters that were closing on us. It was an attempt from me to show my teacher and my classmates that my dad was my legendary savior, and as long as he was with me I was able to face the world, no matter how ugly or scary it got. That was the picture I painted of my father and my young, innocent brain was never able to imagine a life without him. He was Superman, and Zayn believed with all his heart that Superman never dies.

What I didn't know at the time was that Superman had cancer. Yes, my hero hid the fact that he had it right after I was born. He fought that devil for ten years, and I never felt that there was a single threat of something taking him from me. I learned later that when my dad was diagnosed with cancer at the age of forty-three, the doctors gave him six months to live. I was just a baby. He couldn't accept the fact that he was going to leave his boy, that he waited forty-three years for, to grow up without even remembering his dad. My mom told me that he vowed as soon as they got back from the hospital the day of his diagnosis that he would fight his cancer just so he could raise me the way he wanted and to see me grow to the man he always dreamed of calling 'Son.' He never showed any sign of weakness or any sign of sadness. Not only did he show me that he was doing well, but he also believed that, and I think that's what made him survive those ten years of living with the poison that kept eating him alive.

But I guess even the strongest, most courageous man will bow down before the call of death. I was just a kid and thought that every dad's hair fell out at a certain point. I thought that every dad had a hard time breathing when they played catch with their kids in the backyard. I thought that passing out and screaming in the middle of the night with pain was just the way all fathers went through their days. I believed that it was like that for all of my friends and their dads, until that sad, November day. I was in my room painting that picture, and I was really happy with the result and excited about showing it to my dad and seeing his reaction. But I had to wait for it to dry first and was trying to make that happen quickly. So, I opened the window and put the painting on the edge, just so it caught those cold breezes of wind that would rapidly make it achieve perfection in my eyes, just so my dad would love it as much as I did. I was imagining him telling me how great it was and how gifted I was at this and that I'd probably be the next Picasso. Compliments from the most important person in my life could actually make my feel unstoppable, fearless, and confident just because he supported everything I did.

I jumped on my bed and was playing with my Gameboy, killing time, and didn't notice that it had started to rain heavily outside, and raindrops were falling on my dad and me holding hands, fighting the world of evil. I was smiling all along, playing, not realizing that my life, just like that painting, was about to change forever. I remember freaking and running towards my art piece, but I guess I was a bit too late. It was soaking wet, and somehow the rain washed my dad and me from the picture, but it left the monsters there. It was as if the rain knew what was about to happen to me. That it was in my destiny to face those demons alone, and as the rain took my dad away from my painting, life took him away from me that day, too.

I was bummed out, but I didn't care because I knew that

I could start over and do it again, maybe even better. I was really focused on finishing it as fast as I could, only to be interrupted by my mom's calling my name. From the tone of her voice, I realized that something bad was happening. I dreaded answering her call. I slowly walked towards their bedroom, holding my painting and trying to block the fear and negative thoughts that roamed my head. As I walked into their room, I saw my dad laying on the bed, and my mom holding his hand, crying like I never saw before. She looked at me and said, "Come closer, Son, your father wants to talk to you."

I still remember to this day feeling something different in that room. I think death was already there, but it actually had some mercy in between its claws and decided to give us just a bit more time. Dad was sick for a long time, but he looked so much different even from last night. I walked slowly to his side of the bed, looked into his eyes as he slowly held my hand, and tried one more time to fill his gaze with what he held close to his heart.

"Son, you know I love you, right. You know that you are the one gift that I'll thank God for. Well, I'll stand before him soon…"

I was nodding yes, not knowing what to say and trying not to interrupt him. He coughed, and Mom tried to wipe the blood that came out of his mouth. He stopped her, looked at me, and said, "All my life, I tried to show you that I was here for you, but now you have to know that I was willing to prove to my boy that as long as there was blood circulating in my veins he needed no one in this world apart from his father. I loved you, and I will always love you, even after I'm far, far gone…"

I interrupted him and said, "Why are you saying this, Dad? Where are you going?"

"Son, I'm not going anywhere. I promised you before that I would be with you forever, only now you won't be able to see me, but I promise that you will be able to feel my presence. When this life shows you its true face and you wonder, 'Where is my dad? How come he left me to fight this world alone? Does he ever think about me?' you only have to lift your head up high and look towards the sun. And as bright as that would be it wouldn't come close to how much you filled my life with light and love that will travel with me to wherever I'm going."

"But, Dad, I want to see you. I want to see you every day. Dad, I love you, please don't go anywhere. I need you, Dad. Look, I drew a picture of us today, it's for my teacher, Dad. He said draw what makes you happy, and I drew you and me. Look, Dad, it got messed up by the rain, but I swear you are there holding my hand, and we are fighting these monsters like superheroes. Dad, don't you remember that you are my Superman and I'm like everyone human on this earth, I need Superman to protect me."

With tears running down my eyes I looked at my mom who was sitting on the edge of the bed trying to hide how destroyed she was from me.

"Mom, please don't let him go. Please tell him to stay. I'll be better. My grades will be only As, I promise. Dad, I'll make you proud of me, just like I'm proud of having you ..."

"My baby boy."

He said that while his eyes were brimming and he interrupted me, "Promise me, Son, that you will grow up to be the man that I never was. Promise me that you are going to achieve all your goals. Promise me that you will fight for your dreams, and you won't stop until you get what you want, you won't be just another man who lived with no goals to chase and then died regretting he ever existed. You will leave a mark, and you will help others and be the great source of happiness that you are to your parents but also to so many people around you."

"Okay, Dad, I promise you, but you will be here to see that. Dad, my dream is to be just like you. That's all I want to be, there is nothing and no one better than my dad, and I want to be like him because he won't leave me. Right, Dad? You never will, please promise me… please!"

And everything went so quiet, and to this day, I didn't get an answer.

That day, the light of happiness inside me left my body as the soul of the man I loved left his, and the boy who thought that Superman never dies learned about kryptonite and saw the cape of his favorite superhero evaporate and turn into tears, black suits, and strangers trying to comfort him as the ground swallowed the author of the happy life he wished to have. From that day forward, I never believed in faith or destiny, and I just took life day by day, not even thinking about the future. Why do that? We plan and plan, and pray, and wish for things that could just stop existing in the blink of an eye, and I chose to disappear and get lost between thoughts, memories, paper, and people until the lunch break came and I had that one-hour escape that actually helped me recharge my batteries for the rest of day.

Usually, I had lunch with Steven. It kind of became our ritual and was the only time that we sat down together and properly discussed life and things outside of that work bubble of ours. But lately he had been extremely busy with all his new obligations and meetings so I found myself having lunch alone a lot, and to be completely honest, I couldn't complain. Not that I didn't like spending time with my best mate, but I made it fun. There was this balcony in Janice's office that I sneaked to whenever I was alone, as she always left her office and went God knows where to have lunch, and I decided to invade her privacy a little bit because, let's face it, she deserves it. I did it once and got hooked. It was so beautiful and had the most alluring view of the city. I would just sit there, grab my sandwich, put on my music, and lose myself for a couple of minutes and swim wherever the view and the song decided to take me. Thankfully, I never got caught, but I probably would one day will, and I had planned an escape for if that ever happened. If she caught me in there, I would definitely jump from the balcony before I let her reach down into my soul and poison it with her loud screams and venomous humiliation.

I genuinely wonder sometimes about the reason she became like that. What made her this way? Was it a broken heart, or a childhood trauma? Maybe it's loneliness or the fear of dying alone. The only thing I am certain of is that I need not cross paths with that woman.

Life for me became more interesting after I left work every day at five pm and ran headlong to this coffee place that I absolutely loved. I just sat there drinking the heavenly tasting coffee, reading my books, and just enjoying my solitude. I was more than used to being alone. While people would look at this loneliness as a curse, I found it to be more than a blessing. I knew I might be wrong for shutting myself outside of this world, but I was happy like that. I let no one in just so life didn't feel empty after they eventually left. So, I drowned myself using sips from the coffee and words from whatever book I was reading, and sometimes, for a change, I would lift my head up and look around. I'm not a creep but I'm not going to lie when I say I enjoyed looking at people when they weren't aware of it. You could see people laughing, yelling at each other, some of them as silent as me. A few of them looked sad and lost, seeking comfort and relief through puffs of cigarettes. Others were just there, and you couldn't even peek behind the curtain to tell if they were alive or dead. I just saw bodies walking around, but I always wondered, were they going through the same things I was going through? Was it just me, or did life take everyone for a spin into its dark rollercoasters? Everyone was probably writing the story of their lives with its happiness and sadness, and we all prayed that the first one overshadowed the second part of that equation. Today, I felt a different vibe from everyone there. All their eyes were pointed at the TV, and I thought they were watching the news. I didn't pay much attention, but it looked as if people weren't happy with the way things were run in the country and they were taking their protests and demands to the streets, and of course, the government wasn't happy with any of that. It was all politics, and I was right, it was wrong to talk, and for me that was just the most uninteresting thing ever.

I never understood why people would be so interested in following the news. I mean, all you heard was people dying for some reason, disasters happening somewhere, and some other catastrophic event that they would report and make it look as horrible as possible, just for the sake of captivating the audience. Not me, thank you! I wasn't trying to depress myself more than I already was. But to be honest, this time it was very different, and I knew I was contradicting myself, but I got interested in what was happening. So, I stood up and went to Uncle Jamal, looking for an explanation. He owned this place and almost everyone in the area had so much respect for him because he was such a great man. Of course, he wasn't actually my uncle, but I called him that just like everyone else did. I think his son, Ahmed, helped him run the place and they both made those four walls seem like a comfortable resting place to all of us there.

The first time I ever talked with Uncle Jamal was right before I got my job, and I remember it as if it were yesterday. I was over the moon after I got the call and since I had no one to share my happiness with I went there with the biggest smile on my face, ordered a coffee, and sat there thinking that I should spoil myself because I made it into a big company and was definitely on the right path of success. He saw me that day and said, "It's really good to see you finally happy, Son. You come here often but this is the first time I saw circles of happiness floating around you while sipping our coffee, is it that delicious?"

I said, laughing, "Well, your coffee is delicious, sir, there is no doubt there, but the reason I'm happy is because I got this new job in a very foreign company here, and I'm really excited about it. It's going to be a very good step towards my goals and dreams, you know..."

I feel like a fool even thinking about how I felt and how delusional I was, but I guess I didn't know that Office Coordinator there meant print paper and give it to people and hope you don't cross paths with Janice.

He said, "I'm really happy for you, Son, and please, from

now on, call me Uncle. But I want you to promise me that you will always come and drink your coffee here, and I'll promise you that I will always make yours myself and make it as delicious as possible."

"Deal, Uncle, thank you so much for what you said."

From that day forward, every time he saw me he asked me about my job and how was I doing in climbing the ladder of success. I had to lie and thought about never going back there, but I promised the guy, so at least I didn't want to be both a liar and someone who didn't keep his word. So, I chose the lies that came with a smile and laughter every time we talked about work, and I had to pretend that I was still as happy about it as I was that day.

Uncle Jamal was a very positive person and you always saw him with a smile on his face and words of wisdom coming out of his mouth. I approached him now and asked about what was going on, and what they were talking about in the news. And, for the first time, I saw worry and concern in his eyes. He started talking about politics and tried to explain them to me, that the love for power and being at the top of the food chain could be very dangerous, and he ended his speech with, "Son, apparently we are going to be in for an interesting couple of weeks, or maybe months ahead, so you stay safe, okay?"

I smiled and said, "Oh, don't worry, Uncle, politics isn't my thing, and I'm really not interested in getting involved with it right now."

I went back to my spot and sat there not giving whatever he said any importance. I wasn't even listening to what he told me. I held my book and started to dive in between those lines and words it blessed me with. If there was anything I loved about books it was the fact that they disconnected you from this world as long as your eyes kept on devouring their words. It took me to a whole new place, to somewhere you could forget about time and problems, and I felt, for a short period, that I was a part of that story.

Sometimes, I stayed there for hours, and the only thing that brought me back to this world was the sound of Ahmed stacking the chairs after preparing to close the place for the night. I lived alone with no obligations back home, so I could stay as late as I wanted to, but that night it wasn't the case because I was starving and had to eat, so I got up, said goodbye to Ahmed and his father, and left the place wondering what I would have for dinner. Should I cook something or eat last nights' leftovers?

I left there around 8:30 pm and I was on my way home when my phone rang, and of course, without even looking at the caller's ID, I knew it was my mom. Every day she called me around that time, so I answered, laughing, "Mom, right on point…"

"Well, of course, Son, how many sweet, beloved angels do you think I have apart from you?"

"No one?"

"That's my boy. Tell me, Son, how are you?"

"I'm okay, Mom, surviving I guess, like I'm always trying to."

"Oh, I'm sorry, Zayn, you still having problems at work?"

"No, Mom, it's better I swear. I'm used to everyone there, and I made a lot of friends, so it's absolutely better."

"Don't lie to me, Zayn. I know when you do, even though I can't see you."

"No, Mom, I swear, I'm fine, I'm just a bit tired that's all."

"Oh, my poor baby, it's because you're working so hard. Just go home and have some rest, and I'll call you in the morning, okay?"

"Okay, Mom, I'm already walking home."

"By the way, I'm coming to see you soon, so you better get excited!"

"Oh, Mom, please, do you have to say that? I miss you so much, you have no idea."

"I miss you more, my baby boy. I'll see you soon, take care, please. love you."

"Love you more, talk to you tomorrow, goodnight."

Oh, I missed my mom. I hadn't seen her in over nine months. She was just the sweetest, most thoughtful soul God ever created. She loved everyone, and she was so kind to all she crossed paths with, even the people who treated her badly. But ever since she got married to Bassem and I moved here we didn't see each other that often. Her husband was a nice man, and he made my mom happy so the normal feeling that I should have for him was love and respect, right? No, I hated him, and I'm ashamed for saying that. Well, you couldn't like the guy who married your mom after your father died, you just couldn't, no matter how nice he was to me and to her. And no matter how much the poor guy tried to find his way into my life, I kept on shutting him down until I think he finally gave up. Mom got really upset about the fact that we couldn't get along that much. So, me and him made a pact where, in front of her, we acted as if we had no issues between us. We were very chill around each other to the point where she actually believed that I like him. I was good at pretending, so I was very happy with that deal. I couldn't like the man, I just couldn't. Every time I looked at him I remembered my father and couldn't accept that my mom was capable of replacing the man she claimed to love. He was super nice and he tried and tried before with gifts, toys, ice cream, and every possible trick in the book to make me, his stepson, like him. I was stubborn, and it wasn't because he was bad or good, it was because I didn't want anyone to come even close to filling the void that my dad left in my heart. Even though it was a sad feeling, and most people would want to get rid of it, I didn't. It was the only link I had left to my father, but when I saw Mom kind of happy with him we made that pact and it is still standing until this day.

Oh, Mom, the things that she had been through… I remember her heart broke into a billion pieces when my dad died. She'd loved him ever since she was thirteen years of age. Their story was the sweetest, most romantic novel Shakespeare himself wouldn't be able to write.

Mom and Dad were neighbors growing up. To most people it looked as if their marriage was a traditional, arranged marriage, but for them it wasn't. Well, when Mom spoke about it, she always said, "Zayn, God arranged it. Only God can arrange something that beautiful. Living with your father was like living on Earth but our hearts and souls were up there in the heavens that he rests in. Your father is responsible for making me the happiest woman on Earth, and ever since I knew him, he played the most beautiful love symphonies on my heart strings, and he made me feel like I was the most beautiful gift that he had ever gotten. He kept reminding me of that, but deep down, I was certain that he was, and he would always be, God's greatest gift to me. Your father is the definition of the word happiness.

"We used to walk to school together, and he used to wait

for me every day just so we could walk back home. He was my best friend. If anything would upset me he tried his best to make it right. If anyone was mean to me at school he would beat them up, no exceptions. I remember, one time he got suspended for two weeks because our math teacher made me cry in front of the whole class and called me stupid, and your father threatened and promised that he would pay for that. And he did. Your father broke all four windows of his car later that day. He was my savior, Zayn, and I never thought we would end up getting married, but I couldn't imagine my life without him, even for a day. I still remember the moment he told me he loved me and wanted to marry me. It was a hot, summer night, and we were on the roof of your granddad's house playing like kids and laughing our problems off, counting the stars and talking about our plans, and suddenly, he pulled a paper from his pocket, gave it to me, and asked me to read it.

"He was as shy as you are and couldn't tell me how he felt, so he wrote me that letter, which I still have to this day. It wouldn't matter if I had it or not, because I still remember it word for word and it went like this,

Dear God's gift to me,

If you are reading this, then know that I reached a point where I can't keep it inside anymore. Sarah, my life is like a garden, and you are all the flowers that decorate it. Without you, I'll just be an abandoned, hollow shell. I have known you almost all my life, and every day I wish you could see yourself through my eyes. You are the wings I fly with, the air that travels through my lungs. If my life were a puzzle, you would be the last, missing piece that would make the whole thing make sense. I hope that we are never separated, and if we are after this, I hope you know that my heart will never beat for anyone more than it did for you. Look at the stars above us. You will never be able to count them, just like you will never be able to count the number of times my heart screamed out your name and thanked God for sending you to me.

I'm not very good with words and I don't know how to finish this, but what I do know and I'm certain of, is that I love you, Sarah, and I want to spend the rest of my life with you. Will you grant me that honor?"

Her eyes would tear up every time she reached that point of the story. She would look at me, searching for him in my eyes as she finished…

"That was the happiest day of my life. That day I learned what it feels like for your heart to take over your body and make the decision of a lifetime for you…"

That story is probably the reason I didn't, and probably never will, accept Bassem. When I look at her with him I wonder and ask myself, did she forget? Do people forget their feelings, or are they really good at hiding them? She had to move on. She didn't have a choice, but is the fear of ending up alone far greater than the pain of loving for eternity and being loyal, even for the memory of the person who once drew the happiest moments of your life? I didn't appreciate her marrying the man, and I was furious at her when she approached me about it.

I knew it was very selfish on my part, but to this day, after almost thirteen years of being separated from my father, I'm still holding on to the memories and the feelings I shared with him and thought she would do the same. I tried to change her mind, but after a while, I gave up, believing that no love lasted forever, and no promise is held for eternity. I just finished college and was moving out of the house to chase a professional career here, so I accepted that since she liked him, and he was a good man who loved her and took care of her, I wouldn't stand in their way. I thought that him and his two daughters, Meriam and Yasmine, would keep her busy and not let her feel the void that I would leave behind me. It was a win win for everybody.

Two

I opened my eyes to the sound of the alarm. This time, all I kept saying to myself was, "Oh, God I'm really late." I'd hit that snooze button like six times already. I jumped out of the bed, put on my clothes, and left in a rush, running to the bus station, praying that I would catch it in time. I had no other choice, otherwise I might be very late, and that would get Janice involved. I didn't even have a Plan B. Steven wasn't in town for a whole, entire week. They sent him to Greece to handle the company's business there, and I was happy for him because they only do that with the people they plan on keeping and promoting in the company for a long time. He was really excited about it, because he said that he would always have time to chill and relax and I'd probably see that through the pictures he would send me.

I got to the bus station and stood there waiting for it, praying that it would appear behind all the fog that the winter days chose to wear. It was a very cold day, the clouds weren't allowing any sunrays in, and I honestly hated that bleak weather. It was greyish, gloomy and it made everyone feel so depressed. As I was counting the minutes I had left before I started freaking out for real, I felt gentle stokes on my shoulder. I turned around, and it was Madame Jamila. Oh, I smiled straight away, just looking at her. She was one of the sweetest souls that God blessed this earth with. She used to be my French teacher, who I, along with every student she ever had, loved her. Even though she taught me French in primary school, she still remembers me to this day. We used to be neighbors back home and she knows my mom, and through some weird turn of events in her life, she ended up moving here after she retired, and I was blessed with seeing her from time to time. She grabbed my arm, and said, "My dear Zayn, morning, Sunshine. How are you, Son?"

"Hey, Madame, everything is perfectly fine, how are you? How is life treating you, and how is Malik?"

"Oh, I'm okay, Sweetheart, and my son is fine. He moved all the way to Germany to work in a big industrial company there. He's really happy about it, and even though I miss him and don't get to see him that often anymore, I'm happy for his happiness. The only thing that is bothering me is the cold that keeps on digging deep in my bones. I mean, an old lady like me can't handle this amount of degrees below zero," she replied, shivering. "Il fait un temps de chien depuis longtemps ici," she continued in French.

"Oh no, don't say that ma'am, you are still young, and you will always be the most beautiful French teacher that ever existed. Don't worry about the cold, it will pass soon, leaving the place for your favorite season to come bearing flowers, beautiful weather, and the hummingbirds that you spent hours and hours in class lecturing us about how romantic and important they are in the French mythologies."

She couldn't help but laugh really hard at that, and say, "You are the sweetest student I ever had. How is your mom,

Zayn, is she all right?"

"She's fine, you know, just getting busy with whatever life throws at her."

"Oh, that's good to know, please tell her I say hi and hope I'll get to see her soon."

She said that as the bus pulled over and I helped her get in and find a place to sit. There weren't any seats available next to her, but I saw one at the back, so I said, "Well, Ma'am, I hope you have a lovely day. I'm going to go sit there, see you soon."

"Take good care of yourself, Zayn, au revoir."

As I made my way to the seat, I was thinking about the journey that women take through life and couldn't help but think about my life. In fifty years, where would I be? How was my life going to shape itself? Happy or sad? Would I be married, and how many kids would I have? Would I have my own business? Would Zayn be rich or still struggling just to put food on the table? Would people care when I was gone, or would I just be another old guy who lived next door to someone, and most importantly, would I end up alone, and would my last days on Earth be in a nursing home, or next to a loved one? I asked myself all these questions as I sat and looked for my headphones in my pocket, hoping that I could enjoy some music before I went to the battlefield and surrounded myself with stress. I had a playlist ready for the mood I was in consisting of instrumentals from that amazing pianist, Yiruma. I know I'm old school, but that composer's melody actually can cure souls. So, I played it as loud as I could and looked through the window, trying not to think about the future and focusing on how to evade Janice when I arrived at work and how to be as invisible as possible there.

It was the usual ride on the bus, with people coming in at almost every stop. When I got on it was half-full, but now it was really packed, and I felt like the luckiest person on Earth with the seat that I was in. The driver closed the doors, and as the wheels started to roll, we heard a loud knock, and everybody turned towards the door to see a poor girl knocking and making signs to the driver. Surprisingly, he was nice enough to stop and open the doors again, and the poor young woman got in, looking a mess and out of breath from all the running she apparently had to go through to catch the bus. Her hair was all curled up on her head like a bird's nest and she had books coming out of her bag and pencils in her pocket like a five-year-old in a kindergarten class. Since I was sitting next to the door she came in from and there was clearly not a single place for her to sit, the good old boy in me started to talk, "Zayn! Give her your seat! She needs it more than you do. Come on, just get up." I'm not going to lie, I ignored that voice in my head. I was really lucky to have the seat there, the bus was more than crowded and if I got up I was probably going to end up jammed between people, or with my nose shoved in someone's armpit. But then I looked at her, and I felt really bad. She couldn't even move, and she was barely holding on to her bag, so I tapped her on the back, and said, "Hey, you can have my seat."

She looked at me with a smile, "That's very sweet, thank you very much, you're a life saver."

Well, if there is anything about myself I'm sure of it's that I'm a person with almost no social skills at all, especially with girls. She had this very broad smile that was so pretty, to the point where it startled me. I didn't know what to say, so what would a confused Zayn do? He wouldn't even reply. When she said that, I nodded as if I was saying, "Yes, sure. You're welcome, but I'm too cool for words, so I just choose not to talk to you." She looked at me with a look of surprise and I couldn't blame her for that. She probably thought *why is this creep nodding at me instead of speaking like a human being?* So, I looked away, trying to avoid any more eye contact. Oh, this Zayn wasn't good at anything, even the smallest human interactions he couldn't get right. Maybe Janice was right for telling him once that he was worthless. Inside of me, while blaming me for being like me, I couldn't stop saying to myself, "This girl has the most beautiful smile I have ever seen."

She sat down and tried to calm herself from all that running, but only then I realized that this girl not only had a very beautiful smile, but she also had an angelic face that went with it. I thought her smile was actually more beautiful than the music Yiruma was playing in my ears. I looked around and then back at her, and I swear in the bus she was like a lisianthus in a garden full of that poisonous Poet's Narcissus. She had this lustrous coral-black hair that she kept trying to fix as it plunged over her shoulders and two of the most beautiful eyes that gave her a stunningly, soft stare. She was like a little bird looking at the sky, trying to fly for the first time. The only thing you can say when you look at it is, "God created you really well, didn't he?" She had a small, dainty nose and two pretty, heart-shaped lips that covered her shiny, snow-colored teeth, and a two baby, rose-colored cheeks. In the middle of one of them, she had a beauty spot that was like the star in the middle of a midnight sky. I didn't want to keep looking at her, because I felt that I had reached the point of microscopic staring, so I looked at the window, but caught a glance of her reflection on the glass, and I looked at her pulling a little mirror from her bag and trying to fix her make-up.

The bus got to my station, and as I was about to leave, one thought kept on hitting the walls of my brain, *Zayn, you have never seen such divine, charming beauty in your life and you'll probably never see it again, good job looking like a freak that stares and doesn't respond like humans do.* But I didn't care. I blessed my eyes with that charming face of hers and before our eyes met I looked away and just left knowing that this beauty was about to be replaced with God-knows-what waiting for me, because I was late.

I walked in the office and all I saw was Janice roaming around like a hungry lioness waiting for someone to make a mistake, so she could devour their soul and send them into the deepest parts of the unemployment road. I kept my head down and snuck my way in until I reached my station and started pretending as if I had been there from 6 am, working as if the whole company depended on me. I was scared of her, of course, like all the staff here, but deep, deep down I didn't care that much, especially today, because all I kept thinking about was that girl I saw on the bus. All I kept picturing was that heavenly-looking smile she gave me. I think there is something wrong with me. Most people wouldn't give any of what happened to me a second thought, but I don't know, it was either that the girl was a piece of the heavens that attracted people to whatever she did, or I was so sad and lonely to the point where I held on to the smallest things and built and imagined stories based on nothing. I think that's how crazy people become crazy. So, out of fear of becoming crazy, I was just going to say that the girl from the bus was a heavenly spirit, and her smile affected the way my brain worked. Yes, that was better.

For some weird reason, the day went by really fast, and I looked at the time and it said, "You've made it alive, time to go home." I was getting ready to leave when I noticed that Janice's office door was open. Usually, she wouldn't be there until now, so I thought she had left without closing it and I said to myself that I should go and close the door before she finds it like that in the morning and probably thinks someone went in her private sanctuary and that someone needs to be fired. And if she couldn't tell who that someone was, well, it wouldn't matter, she would choose a random person and make an example out of him. I leaned in to grab the doorknob when I suddenly heard Janice's voice talking on the phone. Oh, dear lord, the beast was still there. A round of fear crawled all over my body, and I started backing up, trying not to make a single sound, but I couldn't help but overhear her saying, "Is he okay? Please be honest, is he okay?"

I was intrigued to know what she was talking about, and usually I'm not nosy at all, but it was Janice. For the love of God, she is the black book of evil that no one in the office knew anything about. Her personal life was more than a mystery to all of us. She was the Mackenzie Poltergeist that came to us every day and took us for a tour in the realm of fear and a walk among the dead. So, yes, I did something I'm not that proud of, but I had to get clues so I could try to solve this mystery. I kept on listening as she said, "Oh, God, what should we do? What did the doctor say? Mark, if you lie to me I'll never talk to you again!"

Who is this Mark? I asked myself. Is he her boyfriend? I didn't picture Janice as someone who could love, to be honest. Love is felt with your heart, and emotions run through the rivers of the soul, and I didn't think she had any of those things. One time, our co-worker, Dalia, was engaged and was so happy about it. After her engagement party, she went around the office showing everyone the ring, together with pictures and videos from the ceremony. Janice saw that and didn't appreciate it one bit. She didn't like the couple of minutes the girl was taking away from her desk, so with the help of the black book of torture she so dearly holds in her heart, she sat down on Dalia's chair until she came back, then she said to her face, "Dalia, your services are no longer needed here. We only hire people who are dedicated and work really hard for the eight hours they spend in our company. We do not take playing around and joking during work hours as easily as you might think."

Dalia was shocked and tried to explain, "Oh, sorry, Ma'am, I got engaged and was showing my friends here pictures of the ceremony. It won't happen again."

Janice looked at her dead in the eye and said, "Congratulations, my dear. You're fired."

That's the kind of person Janice is, so I found it very intriguing to know what was going on with her, and as she hung up the phone, I heard her start to cry, which I found even stranger. She has feelings, and that heart can produce tears? I said that to myself knowing that I needed to get out of there before she noticed my presence. I felt that she might need someone to talk to that day, someone who could comfort her and be there for her, but I wasn't brave enough or stupid enough to forget who she was and go in and be that someone. As far as I knew, she could eat me just so she could feel better. Who knows how people like her comfort themselves? *Zayn, you are being mean, the woman isn't the devil for heaven's sake!* So, I just walked as silently as I could to the door, leaving that mystery behind because I knew, one way or another, time would tell. It always does.

Three

You can ask me what the one thing is you hold close and so very dearly to your heart, and the answer would be, without a doubt, pizza! There was a place not far from work that makes the most delicious slices of heaven that I would absolutely die for. Today, after escaping Janice's wrath for arriving late in the morning, and after getting a glimpse at her mysterious life, I felt as if I deserved to spoil myself with that amazing pizza. And since it wasn't far from work, I decided to walk there and enjoy the beautiful weather that the winter night offered. It was cold, but it was a beautiful cold. A freshening breeze of air would strike your face gently every once in a while, and drizzles of rain would lightly touch your skin reminding you that the world outside still wanted you to feel its presence. All of that made me want the pizza more, so I walked rapidly there and made it in a record seven minutes and thirty-four seconds. Yes, I had nothing better to do than count how much time it would take to get there and try to beat the eight minutes I took last time. Loneliness is a scary world, it can drive you crazy, but I chose to cope with its lunacy and tame its madness just so I wouldn't lose myself there.

I stood in line looking at the menu, trying to come up

with the best combination of toppings the place could offer. Luckily, it wasn't packed, and I was really hungry, so I ordered my go-to when I'm starving for pizza, found myself a spot next to the window, and sat down waiting for the sweet ride I was about to embark on. The mood in the place is one of the things that I think makes the dishes they offer taste even better. It's so soothing with the smell that travels around tickling your nose, and the instrumental music they play in the background. I love that type of music, the calm flow that you feel taking over your body and controlling the rhythm of your heart. My favorite instrument is, and will always be, the piano. We used to have one in our old house and to this day the sound and the music it created still visits me from time to time. I think Mom sold it a couple of years ago, but I remember my dad playing it for hours and hours during cold, winter nights similar to this one, and the music was mixed with the sound of the rain and wind that the winter decorated our lives with, creating a picture that an eleven-year-old boy would associate with safety and security, together with happiness and love.

I used to go to sleep to the songs Dad played, and each one felt like a bedtime story that was more beautiful than a million lullabies and more meaningful than a billion stories. His fingers knew their way around the piano, and every time they did, the sound that filled our home took me to a happy place, a place I have been looking for ever since. But today's song brought to my head one single thought, and I hate to admit it, but it was about Janice. I couldn't stop wondering what was happening with her and what would drive a woman as strong as a thunderstorm in the east side of the Andes to breakdown crying. She was the kind of person who I didn't think before was capable of feeling emotions, but now all I kept asking myself was, *is she a good actor like most of us in the world? Does she keep this strong façade for us to see and beneath the surface only God knows what kind of war she is fighting and what kind of pain she is hiding with that unpleasant cruelty?*

The sound of my phone ringing interrupted my line of thought. It looked as if I'd received a message from Steven. It was two pictures with the caption "living life bro." He was hugging two stunningly gorgeous ladies in the photo and it looked as if they were in a pub or a fancy club that if I ever tried to go into I would definitely get thrown out of, so I wrote back:

Did they ask about me? LOL XD

Ha-ha, they did, and I told them if he was here he would have been too shy to talk to you ladies.

You are a mean ladies' man, Steven.

I'll be there on Monday, and I'll tell you all about it. Ciao.

I despised the way he was living his life, and I don't judge, but jumping from one woman to another is the most disgusting thing men do, especially as he had a girlfriend who absolutely trusted, loved and cared about him. I wish I could be like him at times - no, not the cheating part, but I wish I had the courage to talk to girls like he does. If he was in my place, he probably would have had that angel on the bus's number and would have already taken her on a first date and smitten her as he always does with every girl he ever meets. Meanwhile, people like me are only capable of doing the one thing we can do best and that is observe from afar. Sadly, all I do is see my dreams and goals taking the shapes of a tiny butterfly as I bring them to life inside my cortex and let them fly away as soon as I wake up to my reality.

Oh, that angel on the bus... she was probably living her life not even thinking for a second about that guy she met today, the guy who let her sit in his seat and was hating himself for not having the courage to at least ask what her name was. But wait, what was I on about? She probably had a Prince Charming. Obviously, how could someone with that angelic aura not be in a relationship? But still, if she did, he was one lucky man to have a gift like that in his life. She was like that amazing perfume scent that, once you smell it, it will be with you for a long time. Maybe I would see her again and I'd try to convince myself then to have the courage to talk to her, even though deep down I knew that wouldn't happen.

I laughed at that thought as I started to eat the one thing that I would never be afraid to admire publicly and talk so fondly of to anyone – the pizza. It didn't take long for me to devour that delicious dish, and I grabbed my things and headed home saying to myself, *let's face it, Zayn, you will never see her again, so calm down and let her fly away like all the butterflies that come into our lives do.* I was so grateful for the fact that we humans have to sleep, I couldn't wait to go back home and just put all those thoughts to rest. It's the only time I feel that I'm free of these shackles that I walk around in.

Four

I woke up the next day feeling different, without knowing the reason why. As soon as I opened my eyes I felt excitement travel through my body, so I got out of the bed surprisingly faster than I normally do and put on my work clothes. This reminded me that I had to do the one thing I hate the most on this planet and that is laundry. I wish that one day I have enough money to hire someone to do that for me, or just buy something new every day. This resentment to doing the laundry, I think, came from a very horrible experience I had in the laundry room in my building, but that is a story for another time. It involves a rat, our old neighbor, and me not paying that much attention to what I was doing. But let's just say that I almost went to prison doing laundry! Now, let's focus on the excitement I was feeling. All of this was coming from the thought that I slept with yesterday, which decided to wake me up. It was the voice that kept whispering in my ears, "Zayn, the bus... the girl... you will see her again today... hurry up, wake up so you don't miss it."

A part of me believed that, so I got ready as fast as I could and left home earlier than I used to, just so I didn't miss that damn bus. I got to the station and sat waiting patiently for the holy ride to pop up from behind the trees down the road. I took a sip from the coffee that I took with me because, you know, it was too late for me to drink at home, even though I made it here fifteen minutes earlier than usual. But, hey, who cares, I'm going to meet a unicorn in the shape of a flower, in the shape of an angel that looks like a girl, so it was worth it. The only thing that made me kind of nervous was the number of scenarios I kept playing in my head. I was nervous because I was determined to talk to her when I saw her, but I had nothing prepared and zero experience when it comes to situations like this. Should I say, "Hi, it's you! The girl from yesterday."? Or should I play it cool, "I know you from somewhere, right?"

No, no that was too cheesy. I should probably be honest and tell her that she was pretty and I kept thinking about her. *What a dumb idea, Zayn, if you want her to think that you are a creep do that, yes.* Should I call Steven and ask him what to do? No, no I wouldn't. If I did that I'd be hearing about it for weeks. He already considered himself the Messiah of talking to girls. You know what, I'm going to play it cool… probably, and if I don't who cares, I'll never talk to her again. No, I wanted to talk to her again, and again, and again. Oh, God, this was too hard.

The bus arrived, and I needed to stop those thoughts and just get on with it. You know what, whatever happens, happens. I sat where I did yesterday and looked through the window, counting the stops until we reached the place where she got on from yesterday. It was four stops away from mine. I put on my music, looked through the window, watching the buildings we were passing, and kept telling myself, *Zayn, calm down, man, everything is going to be as you planned, don't worry.* One stop, two stops, three stops, and we were there. I watched the door as people got on. I saw an old lady, a woman holding a baby, and a man who was wearing a beanie, and the door closed behind him. I kept staring. Maybe she got on and I didn't see her, but everyone sat down, and it was obvious that there was no angel that day. I didn't know how to feel, to be honest, because I built it up in my head with one outcome, so disappointment was inevitable. I so foolishly believed that I was going to see her, and was going to talk to her, but everything fell apart in a second. Well, I didn't lose anything, right, and as I said, I might not see her again, so I should start believing that now. I felt a bit down, but should you really be upset about losing someone you never even got close to saying hi to? No, so look, Zayn, you are there, it's your stop, so get off the bus and go... Janice is waiting for you.

Oh, Janice, poor old monster that I wished I didn't cross paths with that morning, judging by what I overheard yesterday. I didn't think anybody would want to see her, or even look at her today, because she might consider that today was their day and that they needed to be exiled from her kingdom. I pressed the elevator button, praying that I would have at least a normal day with no horrific, sad encounters, when I felt someone grab my shoulder and scream, "Morning, Zayn! Did you miss me?"

"Not as much as you missed you, Mister. I went to a tanning place called THE SUN."

"I knew you were going to say that. Well, this is a Windsor tan, you illiterate dummy!"

"You can call it whatever you want, I'll call it 'Steven decided to have the same color as his shoes.'"

"You won't believe how much girls dig this!"

"Yeah, of course they do, we are talking about you, Steven, and girls always dig whatever you do!"

"Damn right they do, shut up and push the twenty-second-floor button please, I need to go say hi to the guys there."

The elevator was stopping at almost every floor. We reached mine and people were coming in, so we kept quiet and Steven started talking to them about his trip. And, of course, he made it sound as if he was solving the world's most complicated problems and that he helped keep the company alive. Everyone was agreeing with him, and I had a smile on my face through all of it, as I knew what he did and how much work he put into the trip. But I guess I'll never be able to understand guys in suits, it was as if the higher you got on the success ladder, the more bull-crap you were able shove down other people's throats with them enjoying it.

I gave Steven a tap on the shoulder.

"See you later, buddy..."

"Will we have lunch together?"

"Yeah, sure, twelve thirty, same place?"

"I'll be there."

The first thing I heard as I exited the elevator was Janice's screams and roars scaring every human soul on that floor. It was 8:30 am and one would have thought that nothing could have gone wrong yet for her to be mad at, but I swear, I think she was screaming at Ali for a mistake he made three days ago, but she didn't feel satisfied the first time she yelled at him. So now it was the second round. Poor guy, she had ruined his day already. There was me thinking that Janice could be affected by whatever she was going through, but it looked as if she was wearing the mask of the vicious figure she had built over the years. So, I decided that it might be good for me to keep away from her line of sight and disappeared in my station, praying that time would fly. Thank God it did, and I found myself in the elevator with a bunch of people about to take our one-hour lunch break.

I made it to the restaurant before Steven and sat down thinking what would be better to eat, the kebab sandwich or the chicken one. They were both delicious, but I thought I'd let Steven decide, we always order the same thing and it's usually one of those two.

"Hey, buddy!" said Steven, as he sat down in front of me.

"Hello, I'm sorry, I'm waiting for Steven, sir, my friend. I don't know if you know him, but he's a human being with normal human skin color not an orange one."

"Would you stop it about this damn tan man!"

I was just getting on his nerves for fun, it wasn't actually that bad, or that orangey or weird, but it was the one thing I didn't expect him to do, so I would probably keep teasing Mr. Perfect like he always did to me.

"Okay, okay, I just have one more joke!"

"Fine, go ahead."

"Knock, knock…"

"Really, Zayn, a knock-knock joke, what are you, twelve?"

"I said knock, knock, do you want me to let it go or not?"

"Okay, fine, who's there?"

"Orange."

"Orange who?"

"Orange is the new Steven color!"

I was on the floor with tears in my eyes, even though the joke wasn't that funny, but the way he looked at me made me laugh even harder, and he loved the show I referred to, so it was all on point.

"Okay, okay it's a truce for now. I won't make any more jokes about it, I promise."

"Finally, man, about time you grew the hell up."

"Yeah, sure, so tell me, how was your trip? From the pictures you sent me I could tell that crazy things happened, so tell me everything!"

"Dude, it was amazing! Well, first of all, the work I actually went to do I finished in the first day, signed a bunch of papers and met some people, and that was it. I cleared my schedule for the actual work I had in mind, and for the next five days I made sure to enjoy the living hell out of that beautiful weather they had there."

"Yeah, really! What did you do? Did you go swimming?"

"Well, I rented a car and went around the city to buy a couple of gifts for Mary, just so I wouldn't hear about how I forgot about her when I came back. And, as I was roaming around the streets of this chic neighborhood they had there, I discovered this placed called Safe Haven. Dude, it's the best club I have ever been to, and you know I've been to a lot. It was on a hill and had this amazing view of the sea, and everyone there was good looking, even the bouncer and the bartenders looked like models."

"Yeah, right!" I said, laughing.

"I swear, man! I lie to you not, Zayn. Just let me finish, okay? I went in and knew I had to bring my A game, so I did that, and, of course, when I bring my A game you know there will be casualties, bro."

"Oh, for God's sake, you are not Casanova, man, relax with the metaphors!"

Steven was laughing so hard as he finished, "You are probably jealous you weren't there. I met two beautiful

Russian girls who were there on holiday, Darya and Ludmila. Dude, don't get me started on Darya. That girl is freaky. She is the prettiest girl I ever saw."

"Dude, you say that about every girl you see!"

"No, I mean it this time, bro. She was out of this world pretty; you have no idea..."

"Did you guys decide what you are you going to order?" asked the waiter, interrupting Steven.

I said, "I'll have the kebab sandwich and a soda, medium-size, please."

"You know what, I'll have the same, just no tomatoes and no onions for me, please."

"Steven, tomatoes are good for you, you should start eating them!"

"Stop it, Mom, you know what's good for me? Ludmila is good for me. She is this darkhaired lioness who took me for the ride of my life there, Zayn. I did things. Things that might be a nightmare or a fantasy for people like you, things you wouldn't dream about doi..."

I interrupted him, laughing, "Really, Steven, back to quoting that movie again? I thought you let go of that."

"Well, Ludmila reminded me of everything. She made me even question my life, dude."

"Oh, dear! Lord have mercy on your soul. Steven, look at me. What about Mary, didn't you think about her while you were doing all of this?"

"I swear you sound just like my conscience. We are men. We have needs and you know that. I did think about her that's why I bought her that $3200 bag. Why did I do that you ask? Because I'm a good boyfriend, Mister-Did-You-Think-About-Mary, and I was having fun, nothing serious, so stop complicating everything, please."

"Steven, you're my friend, my best friend, but there are times when I wish I could punch you and knock the dumbass living inside you out."

He burst out laughing and said, "You can try, but I promise, the only one who would be knocked out is you, pretty boy," he said, flexing his arms at me.

"Okay, cut the jokes, tell me about you. What happened with you? Anything interesting?"

"Nothing interesting, Steven, you know me. If you leave for a week or a month it will be the same. I'm living in a circle. God only knows when I'll be leaving it. The only thing out of the ordinary that came into my life is that I overheard Janice yesterday talking on the phone. Dude, she was crying and was very emotional, like I have never seen before."

"Well, well!" said Steven. "Looks like the beast has a heart after all."

"I think someone in her family might be sick."

"Does she even have family? I thought Loch Ness monsters lived alone!"

I burst out laughing, "Dude, stop. Don't be that mean."

The waiter brought the food, and the sandwiches looked so delicious we started eating, and as I took my first bite looking out the window, a bus drove by, and I remembered the girl from the other day and said to myself, *Should I tell Steven about it? After all, nothing happened, and he can't make that much fun of me for it.* I looked at him and said, with no introduction, "Steven, I met this girl, right, and...

He immediately started choking on his sandwich and looked at me, saying, "Oh, God. Oh, God, Zayn, don't drop news on me like that. Tell me, did you marry her already?"

"I swear, if you don't get serious right now, I'll never tell you anything from now on. And it's nothing like that, you idiot, just wait till you hear the rest of the story…"

"Okay, fine, I'm all ears."

"So, I was on the bus the other day, and this beautiful creature got on four stops away from my house. Steven, I have never seen anything like her beauty, she looked like a painting drawn by God himself. She was late, apparently, so I stood up and gave her my seat, and good God, when she smiled at me I felt I was lifted from this earth, went all the way to the sacred paradise, smelled the most beautiful flower there, and drank from the beauty fountain. As I came back to the moment, I froze like I always do, Steven. I didn't say anything. I just looked away like a retard. So, I thought I'd talk to her the next day when I saw her again, but that never happened. She never got on again, and it looks as if I'll never see her again.

Steven looked at me with the 'I feel sorry for you' face, because this isn't the first time I dropped my epic 'I want to talk to a girl' story fail on him, and believe me, I had a lot. It's not that I like every girl I see. No, it's just this fear of rejection, or whatever it is I have, that cripples me and makes me unable to even say, "Hi, you are very pretty."

"Zayn… brother, when will you have the courage to chase something you really want? And I'm not talking only about this girl here. I'm talking about you in general. It's like you have put yourself in a cell, closed the door, shoved the keys in your pocket, and pretended you can't get out of there. You are way over-qualified for the job you are doing, but somehow you can't seem to see that, and you can't see that you need to do something about it. All the girls you ever meet, Amal,

Lina, and Mariam to name a few, all of their stories are like the one you just told me. 'I saw a girl, I liked her, she seemed so nice, I really wanted to say hi, but I never did. The end.'

"You are the brother I never had, and I wish I could help you out, but what can I do? God only helps those who help themselves, so please, Zayn, please, I think it's time for a change."

I hated every word he said, only because I knew he was right. I put down the sandwich that I no longer wanted to eat and just looked at him as he finished.

"I know this hurts, and I know you think that I'm a lady's man who can't tell right from wrong, and that I ruin everything I touch, but when it comes to this you know I'm right."

"You are, Steven, you are, but..."

I was interrupted by his phone ringing, and it looked as if it was important, so I said, "Pick up, Steven, it's all right."

"... oh, really, we don't have to come back? Okay, I'll go pick my car up then, I don't want to leave it the parking lot there, okay, thank you!"

"That was security from work. It looks like there is a march heading to the parliament building facing ours, so they said for security reasons we shouldn't go back as they are closing the whole building for the day."

"A march. What march?"

"Dude, I've been away for a week, and I know what's going on in the country more than you do. People are manifesting against the president here. It has been going on for a while, and the police aren't making it very easy on them, so who knows what is going to happen. I'm going to get my car because it's not safe there, if it gets violent they are going to destroy everything on sight. Catch up with you later?"

"Yes, sure, we'll talk later, no worries. Just be safe."

Steven ran back to the office as I paid the bill and headed home, wondering what was going on in the country. I heard before that there was something not quite right here, but I never gave it a second thought. I mean, I'm really not into politics. I don't follow the news and I don't think I'm going to start now. But I know someone who is good at analyzing everything, Uncle Jamal. I needed to get there fast so I could make sense of all of this.

Everyone on the street looked confused and a little scared, which made me worry more, so I texted Steven to find out if he made it there or not, and thank God, he replied fast, saying he was on his way home. So, I picked up my phone and called my mom, "Hey, Mom, how are you?"

"Zayn, love, I'm good, how are you? I was just about to call you, are you home? Are you okay? Please tell me you are home. I've seen the news and it looks like there is a march about to take place, and who knows how the police are going to treat the people there. Go back home right now please."

"Mom, I'm okay. I just wanted to call you before you got worried. I'm okay. I'm heading home right now, please don't worry about me, I'm safe."

"Okay, Son, go! Go now, text me when you get there."

Suddenly, things became intense, and I could hear police sirens everywhere closing down on the block, so I almost ran, and I made it to Uncle Jamal's café. What made it more serious now was that the place was closed. Uncle never, and I mean never, closed the café, but luckily, he was there standing in front of his place, making sure that everything and everyone was safe. As soon as he saw me he ran towards me and screamed at me, "What are you doing here, Zayn?"

"I came to see you, Uncle. I was wondering what was going on. Everyone suddenly became really scared, and I needed an explanation so, of course, I came running towards your café. Why are people protesting, and why is everyone so on the edge?"

"Zayn, go home, it might become really dangerous for young, non-religious males like you. We will talk tomorrow, okay. I'll explain everything. I told you, you should watch the news more often."

"What's wrong with people like me, sir?" I said, laughing, knowing that his answer will probably be more obscure news and terms that I know nothing about. "Now I have you, why would I need the news?" I said that waving goodbye.

"We will talk tomorrow, Son, be careful."

A dark cloud of fear, or maybe uncertainty and doubt took over the city, and faces that never took down the smile they had been decorated with for years started to shrink and show a face of panic and despair.

I decided to take a shortcut on the way home and avoid all the places where I might expect things to get a bit dangerous. So, I turned on Fourth street, and, for some weird reason, our local bookstore was still open. Well, it's not just a bookstore, it's kind of a bookstore/library, where you can either rent a book or sit there and read it while drinking the only thing they serve there, which is their hot chocolate delicacy. I used to read books a lot. It was one of my favorite things in the whole, entire world. But ever since I started this job, I didn't even have time to live the lonely, boring life I used to have, let alone read books. It actually makes me sad when I think about it, because books were the oxygen masks that I breathed through when life got really hard. It was something

I gave up on, just as I gave up on painting. When I was a kid, every time I held a brush and started drawing and filling those lines with colors that mostly didn't make any sense, it took me on a wild trip just like the trips I took with every line I read. They gave me wings to escape the sad reality I was living and made me lose track of what was actually going on around me.

You know what, Zayn, since today was an unusual day, you need to do something unusual, something you love and haven't done for so long. I was going in, and my plan was to go through all the books they had there, choose one, and spend the next couple of days reading.

I pushed the door and went in, and as usual, Gabriella was on the front desk. As soon as she saw me she said, "Oh! Look who's here. Zayn, where have you been, how are you?"

"Hey, Gabi, I'm okay. You know how life is, sometimes it separates us from the things we hold close and dear to our hearts."

"No, Zayn, nothing is as important to our human spirit as holding a book and diving in the pages of glorious knowledge it offers. You know what, I'm mad at you, and you are going to make up for the time you lost. Go upstairs, there is a new collection of all sorts of books that I'm sure you are going to fall in love with. You need to take at least three books home with you. Read them as soon as you can and come talk to me about the waves you rode with every page you turned. Go! Why are you still standing here?"

Gabi is such a sweetheart. She is too generous with words to the point where she could make you believe and do whatever she wanted you to do. She is probably eighty-years-old, and to this day she has never stopped spreading the mesmerizing scent her books have to offer.

I went upstairs, started going through every title they had, and was happy with the variety of books they offered. The atmosphere the store had was amazing. It was so quiet. Only a couple of people were there, and you could see clearly that everyone was in the little world of imaginary tales they read. What made it even more beautiful was the sound you heard at almost every corner of people turning pages of stories yet to be unveiled. A cover caught my eye. It had the word *Fate* for a title, so I grabbed it and started checking it out.

"Zayn, I'm so sorry to say this, but we are going to close the store, the protestors are coming this way. Gabi is afraid they might invade her store, but she says if you want to stay, please do. You can leave after they are gone, and she is offering our famous hot chocolate for free for those who decide to stay and 'defy the gloomy clouds politics are bringing to our homes' - her words, not mine."

"Okay, Naim, I'm in. You had me when you said free hot chocolate."

"It's coming right up, Zayn."

What a sweet kid. I think Naim is related to Gabi somehow, because he keeps calling her Auntie. He works with her here and helps her take care of the place. Honestly, I didn't want to leave and go back home only to worry and stress myself over whatever was going on in our streets, and I particularly thought that the place was extra beautiful, and the books were so charming today. So, there was no harm in staying, but I had to do something important before anything else, and that was text my mom telling her I got home safe and sound and she had nothing to worry about. I had to lie, if I told Mom that I was in a bookstore and there was some sort of a riot going outside its doors she was probably going to freak out and scream at me until I did what she asked, so a tiny lie wouldn't hurt and it would save both of us.

I dived back into the book I held, and the first line was, "Fate will decide how your life will be painted, it's either black and white or a rainbow of colors and emotions, but if you look closely there is beauty in both..."

That was a captivating line because it had me wondering what beauty the writer saw in black and white. I was intrigued to know his approach to this whole fate thing. I don't believe in fate. I believe that every action we take has a consequence, and who ever believes that fate will change their life at any point is like someone believing that they only need a bit of luck to win the lottery and flip their lives upside down. Come on, life is so much harder than that. I started debating the book even before I read it, so I knew automatically that it was a good one to pick and I was going to enjoy every word of it. I felt a tap on my shoulder. It was probably Naim bringing me that amazing hot chocolate, so I turned and said, "Naim, it's about tim..."

Oh, my God... it wasn't Naim... it was the angel from the bus looking at me, holding a bunch of books and with a smile that was more beautiful than a raindrop gently touching the surface of a rose, making it reflect the outstanding colors that filled its petals.

She said, "Hey, stranger..."

Five

I felt as if my brain hadn't processed the information it was receiving correctly. I didn't even know how to feel the storm of emotions filled with reactions that I was afraid to let out. Maybe, all of this happened because I wasn't used to seeing this type of delicacy up close, but I had to say something before I looked like the creep that I am. So, I stopped staring and said, "Hey, you, do I know you from somewhere? You look familiar."

DO I KNOW YOU FROM SOMEWHERE? Really, Zayn. Really, is that the best thing you have? The girl standing in front of you is probably the only thing you have been thinking about for the past couple of days and you are asking her that. Call your mom, Zayn, ask her if she dropped you as a baby.

"Yeah, we met on the bus maybe a week ago, and you were so sweet and gave me your seat, don't you remember?"

"Ah, yes, I remember now, you looked as if you needed it more than I did that day."

"I did. I was so late and had an exam early in the morning, and my alarm clock wasn't loud enough to wake me up the first fourteen times it rang…"

"Oh, look who's so lazy to get up even when they have to.

You're lucky you had me that day otherwise you would have been in so much trouble," I said, laughing.

"Don't blame me, stop laughing, and I know, thank you so much, but it's not my fault that my bed is holding on to me and never wanting to let me go."

"Yeah, right, blame it on the bed, Miss..."

"Farah, my name is Farah..."

"Hi, Farah. I love sleep so much... I'm Zayn."

She laughed as she said, "Would you please stop it. I blamed myself enough for it, believe me."

"Okay, I'll stop teasing you if you tell me what your favorite book is."

"Wow, that's a very hard question, sir. I have a collection of books that I absolutely adore, but if I had to choose one I'd probably go with Paolo Coelho's, *The Alchemist*. I don't know why, but that book with its story spoke to me in a way no other book could. Do you know it?"

"I heard that title before, but I never got around to reading it. What do you like about it?"

"What's not to like? Everything is amazing in that book. The plot, the way the writer drew the story, and the best part was that the book had me believing in fate and opened my eyes to the truth I was too blind to see. And that is, if something was meant to be yours it will be, and the universe will collide and conspire to bring it to your feet. You just have to take the first step towards it."

"I see that you are a strong believer in fate."

"Of course, I am. Sometimes, things happen in our life and we think it's out of pure luck, and we think that it has no meaning behind it. But gradually it will have more of an impact on our life than we could ever have by planning and planning, and worrying if the plan didn't go right."

"Well, I don't!" I said that very firmly. "I believe in hard work paying off and in chasing something until the end. Knowing what you want and what you don't, and not relying on something that might or might not happen."

"You are wrong, my friend, time will prove that to you, you will see..."

"I will definitely see... the fact that I'm right," I said, laughing as I looked at her reaction, so I added, "You know what I would never doubt?"

"What?"

"I would never doubt that the hot chocolate Naim is bringing is the most delicious thing ever."

"Oh, my God, you think that too. It's more than delicious, every sip of that holy cup is a trip to the other side of paradise."

Naim's appearance was perfectly timed because I needed a couple of moments to pinch myself and realize that what was happening now wasn't a dream and was a part of my reality. I was talking to her, and it was going great. I didn't know how, but it was. I'm a very awkward person with very weird social behavior when it comes to talking to strangers, but with her, it didn't feel that way.

We took our drinks and sat down on this weird, yet comfortable, vintage sofa Gabi had in the corner next to the fireplace, and just like the flames giving the room a warm, lovable red color, every word that girl spoke was a melody gently playing its way around the place. She had this way of talking patiently about everything and moving her hands around, which made her look like an orchestra maestro captivating everyone with every move he took. I have never seen something more beautiful than the smile she had on her face most of the time, and I never thought that I'd say this one day, but I think fate made us cross paths again, and that shook my belief about something I had always believed in.

If every human being on the planet was reduced into one book that talked about them, hers would be the most interesting one, and it became even more interesting every time I asked something. Her answers were just like scientific discoveries that lit the world for their readers and for future souls to ever come across that prophecy.

"Do you want to play a game?" I said.

"Yeah, sure, what type of a game?"

"A very simple one. We ask each other three questions and the answer has to be completely honest no matter what or how personal the question is..."

"Oh, sounds interesting, I have never done this before, but why not. Since it's your idea, you go first."

"Okay, number one, what was the happiest moment of your life?"

"Where do I start? No, I'm kidding. What if I said I have never felt the happiness that would make me consider it as the happiest moment of my life? I've had many happy moments, don't get me wrong. For example, when I did well in my finals, or when Dad bought me a red bike for my eleventh birthday, or maybe when I sang and played the piano in a school play and the whole crowd stood up and cheered for me, even though I knew that my voice wasn't that good. You see, the way I look at happiness, it's like something we chase, but as soon as we catch it, it slips right away and the chase starts again. I don't know if that makes sense, but it feels like the happy moments in our life are very short compared to the sad ones, but we never have to stop that pursuit. I guess it's what makes us all keep going."

"I completely agree with you there, you were taking the words out of my mouth, I swear. Now it's your turn. Go ahead, ask me anything."

"If you were to wish for one superpower, what would it be and why?"

"Definitely time travel... I'd also like being able to fly, but if I had to choose only one I would go with time travel. I would love to go back in time to when life was a lot easier. Don't you feel that the world we live in now is full of stress, failure, and pain? I would go back to when it was very simple to smile and sleep at night, and I would go back to when my father was still alive and relive every moment I spent with him over and over again, and scream at him every second of every day how much I loved him. Oh, no, now when I think about it, maybe if I had to choose one superpower it would be being able to heal anything, yes that, please, I would..."

"Zayn, I'm so sorry about your father," she interrupted me with the most merciful look a human being could ever have. "I'm sorry, I didn't know..."

"No, please don't be, it's okay, stuff like that happens to millions of people around the world. I was just unlucky being one of them, but come on, let's not turn this into a sad moment, let's move on with our game. It's my turn now, right? What is your biggest fear, Farah?"

"I'm afraid of a lot of things, but maybe the one thing that terrifies me the most is the idea of growing old doing something I completely hate. I'm saying that because I'm studying computer engineering at university and absolutely hate it. I hate every single line of code I write every day. I hate every instruction I learn and every time I press that stupid compile button. I don't even know why I'm studying. I'm not even that good at it. Zayn, why are you laughing?"

"I'm sorry, I wasn't. It's just that I also studied computer science, and I know you are going to hate me for saying this, but I freaking loved it, every single course I took was interesting for me."

"Okay, I'm going to ignore what you just said and keep answering your question, Mister-I-Love-Algorithms. It's not just about my studies. I have the feeling that even though many things are going forward in my life, I find myself until this day, a twenty-two-year-old woman with no true purpose. I don't even know what I want and that terrifies me. It's like being in the middle of nowhere, with no one to help you, and you still have to find a way out. Tell me, isn't that scary?"

"It is, believe me, I know. But don't worry, eventually you will find a way out, you're not alone feeling like this. I think ninety percent of all humans experience that feeling of being lost at a certain point in their lives, but right now I need you to promise me something, promise me that you won't stop the search, and you'll never cave to what the reality throws at you until you really find your purpose in this world."

"You are so sweet, Zayn, I promise I won't."

"Pinkie promise?"

"You're so funny. Yeah, sure."

We pinkie promised over it like little kids, with both of us smiling, looking at each other, saying to ourselves, "I can't believe I'm pinkie promising a stranger in the middle of a bookstore with a riot taking place outside."

"My turn now, Zayn. What is the one thing that you wish you could change about yourself?"

"Nothing, I'm flawless, girl."

She burst out laughing as I finished. "No, for real, there are a lot of things I wish I could do something about. Maybe the one thing that bothers me the most is the fact that I'm a very unsociable person. I don't have many friends and I don't reach out to many people. You know what, let me tell you a secret that I probably shouldn't, but I'm going to anyway. When I saw you on the bus, I really thought that you were the most beautiful girl I had ever seen, and it startled me when you were super nice and said thank you. I couldn't even reply to you. I just nodded like an idiot, and I know that it came off rude, so I want to take advantage of this moment and apologize for that."

Her face took the color of a red flower on a beautiful spring day and there it was, that smile I saw on the bus appeared again.

"Zayn, you are so sweet I swear to God, and believe me, you don't have to think like that. I've known you for what, thirty minutes, and I enjoy talking to you so much, just as I'm sure everyone in my place would, you are a delight, and I hope you see that."

"I don't know what to say, Farah. That's the sweetest thing anyone has ever said to me... thank you."

"Don't thank me, ask me a question, it's your turn."

"Okay, I have a question, but if you don't feel comfortable answering it feel free not to. How is your heart? And please tell me I don't have to explain that question."

She laughed and said, "Oh, Zayn, you make me laugh asking silly questions like this. My heart is perfectly fine right now, as it's not beating for anyone except me, and that is one way of achieving happiness in this world. But, unfortunately,

I learned that after a struggle trying to force it to beat for someone who didn't deserve it, the game that we play with our hearts is a very dangerous one. Sometimes, it can be fun and exciting like drugs. It will fill every part of your body, making you happier than everyone else, but sometimes it will shove you down to the ground making you regret not playing it in a completely different way. I really like the way you asked the question, stranger. Smooth!"

"Well, 1 thank you, dear Farah. I work on my questions. Now it's your turn for the final question."

"Okay, let me make it count. If you were to die tomorrow what…"

"Hey, Zayn, Gabi says that it's better for you guys to leave now because it's getting dark outside, and the protests are over. It's safer for you to go now before it gets really late and who knows what might happen."

"Oh, really, that fast, we have been here for what, forty-five minutes?"

"No, Zayn, you guys have been here for four hours now, everyone else left except you two."

We looked at each other, surprised by the fact that we hadn't noticed time flying. I helped her with her coat, got the book in my hand, and we started walking towards the door.

"You still owe me one answer, stranger!"

"Well, if you don't mind, we can meet again, and I'll answer it with a very complicated answer for you to analyze."

"I kind of like that, here give me your phone."

She typed in her number and saved it under 'Farah, the girl from the bus'.

So, I laughed at her doing that and said, "Since you did that, let me type in my number too, and save it the way I want…"

She laughed as I saved mine under 'Zayn, the stranger from the library.'

"That's too long, Zayn, it won't let you save it."

"Oh, don't be silly," and I pressed Save, "See, it's all done."

And we said goodnight, laughing as our houses were in opposite directions, and I walked home for the first time in my life carrying with me a reason to smile when I lay my head on the pillow at night.

As I reached for my keys and unlocked my door, I received a text saying: *It was beautiful talking to you today, stranger.*

So, I replied, *It was more than beautiful looking at you for four hours, Farah. See you soon.*

You are definitely sleeping with a smile on your face tonight, Zayn.

Six

Have you ever had a dream that was so real and alluring, making it hard for you to tell reality from fiction upon waking up? Well, I have been living that beautiful dream for days now, but I'm living it with my eyes wide open.

A week passed from that day in the library, and a new blessing came into my life, a new friend I spent most of my days talking to. Suddenly, the twenty-four hours I used to hate were not that gray anymore. When I wake up in the morning, now I do it with a smile on my face, running to my phone, checking to see if I'll find a beautiful melody in the form of words that will brighten up my day. Suddenly, I stopped complaining so much about everything negative that I was going through, and rather focusing on the moments of laughter we lit our nights with. The best part of all this was the fact that getting to know Farah didn't feel like getting to know someone for the first time. I find it very hard to explain it even to myself, but the closest thing to an example is to imagine that you are watching your favorite movie, imagine that feeling after you finished it and how it overwhelmed you, maybe with joy or tears from how it good it was. Now imagine forgetting all about it for years and after a very long time you come across it again and you watch it one more time. You fall in love with it again, only this time every scene comes to you with a flashback, making you remember how you felt about it before. But now it's blessing you with twice the pleasure and enchantment.

It wasn't, "Hi, we just met, let's get to know each other." But it felt like meeting up with an old friend, meeting up with your long-lost best friend who completely gets you without having to explain your opinion, who completely agrees with you on most of the crazy ideas for the future that you never shared with anyone. Your best friend who takes words out of your mouth and shares most of your dreams and goals. Someone who is so passionate about life just like you are, someone who came into your life when it was an untouched coloring book and started coloring it page by page, giving it this harmonious rainbow of colors that eventually is giving life to it.

The country we lived in was filled with hatred and hostility as the people protested every day against the government and the president. Now, when you walked the streets all you saw was fear spreading from one home to another. Everyone feared what the future was holding for us. If I had been alone during this period, I probably would have gone crazy from how much stress and horror was spread and poured into our ears, but I had her and that served as an oxygen mask that breathed me back to life every day, getting me out of the dusty reality we were living in.

Even though I was able to suppress the negativity around me, I couldn't escape it. The way things escalated from small protests here and there to full-on violent clashes everywhere, frightened me and it made living here more stressful and difficult.

It doesn't even feel safe to open the windows of your own home. The view from almost each house was either burning car plastic or tear gas flying everywhere. It's impossible even for someone like me, who has very small interest in politics, to escape but I was lucky – I was lucky to have her.

My life was lit from the inside out, and flares of joy and delight flew in all of its corners, but nothing is ever perfect and there were some places that the light couldn't reach, and some darkness could not be lit no matter what. The person responsible for this lightlessness in my life was, with no doubt, that woman, Janice. Every day at work she still played the role of the world's greatest menace, and today wasn't any different. Luckily, I wasn't the victim today, but I had to watch the massacre take place and the poor prey was our co-worker, Karim. The poor guy got his pride crushed, and it probably killed his appetite, as it happened when everyone was leaving for lunch. The mistake that brought this hellfire punishment on his head was the fact that he forgot to CC her in one of the emails he sent out to one of our clients. I think she didn't just punish him for the mistake he did, but he took the blame for everything that wasn't working here. Lately it had been stressful for everyone here, especially the guys in charge. Since the protest started last month, the high-ranked partners were thinking about closing down the company here and moving it somewhere else, somewhere stable. For a business this size, closing for a day is a huge loss and the owners can't sustain conditions like this. They were trying to keep this move a secret, but Steven told me because they requested him to move alongside a couple of people who they considered essential to the well-being of the company. He asked for my opinion, and I asked him if we can discuss it over lunch, same spot as last time, also so we could make up for the one the protests made us finish early.

I got there first as I always did, and Steven, despite usually being late, wasn't so far behind.

"Hey, Zayn, what's up, how are you?"

"Hey, Steven, yeah I'm good, better than you I think. You look like shit. What's going on?"

"Yeah, I do, don't I?" he said, and followed it with a long stare at the floor as if he was waiting for someone to carry the weight on his shoulders for a while.

"Buddy, you are freaking me out. Talk!"

"I slept in my car last night. I tried to, at least, but my eyes didn't rest for even a second. Mary and I had a huge fight, and I couldn't take it anymore, so I left."

"What happened, Steven, did she kick you out?"

Steven looked down as he tried to keep it together and said, "Yeah, she did. I'm lost, man. She found out about the damn Russian girls, and I couldn't even deny it. She went through my phone and the pictures were right there proving how stupid I was. I wish I could take it back. I wish I could take everything back, but I guess it's too late. When I left, she couldn't even look at me. She didn't even say a word, her finger pointing at the door, and her tears were the last thing I saw. I don't know what to do, if she leaves me I have nothing here, Zayn, nothing to breathe for. I feel sick and just can't believe that I caused her that much pain. I don't think I would give me a second chance, let alone the girl who loved me with all her heart and kept up with my nonsense just to have her pure heart tainted by my presence in it. I had a meeting today with the CEO and all the partners and they are officially moving the company to Europe, probably France, or Italy. They are sorting out the legal side of the movement as we speak, and the country that is going to facilitate that is the one they are going with. I'm one of the few they attached to the company so…"

"Steven, stop talking about work, I don't give a damn if this company gets burnt to the ground. I don't even know what to say. You dropped this on me like a bomb; we need to try to salvage your relationship with Mary."

"There is nothing left to salvage, man! I saw it in her eyes, and I just have to live with that."

"You know what, you're right. Let's get out of here, I don't feel like eating anything anymore."

We walked out of the restaurant as I continued, "You are my friend and I know you are hurt now, but…" I looked at him and tears started to fill his eyes, so I calmed myself down a bit and knew that he was broken to pieces and there was no point in blaming him anymore. I put my hand on his shoulder and said, "We need at least to try to get you back together with Mary before you talk about you leaving. I don't know if she will forgive you but we need to try. I'll swing by the house today and try to talk to her. Finding out that you have been living a lie, it isn't easy for anyone to process and forget something like that, most people don't recover from that, and the wound never heals, so prepare yourself for the worst."

I had never seen Steven that sad in my entire life, and I never thought that he cared that much about Mary. To be completely honest, I kind of expected this to happen a long time ago, but if there was anything I was sure about, it was that no one would ever love him as much as she did. And that was the only argument that could back me up in the conversation I'd have with her, so maybe, just maybe, she would find a place in her heart that still beats for him and could at least give him a second chance.

"Thank you, Zayn, you are always there for me. Someone like me doesn't deserve good people like you in my life."

"Stop talking like that or you'll never see my face again."

"No, please don't say that. Okay, forget about me, tell me, how are you? Anything new and exciting you can talk to me about?"

How unfair would it be to tell someone who is having the crisis of his life and apparently losing the person he loves the most that you found the author of the happiest dreams you ever had? I kept my mouth shut, and we just kept talking about random stuff in a desperate attempt on my part to try to make him not think about the scary days waiting for him.

"Buddy, keep your head up, okay?" I said, as we walked back to work. "Here's the key to my apartment, wait for me there and I'll go talk to Mary after we leave here. Let's not worry about something before it happens."

"Thanks, Zayn, I don't think I can ever thank you enough for this."

"Don't thank me. Promise me that if she does forgive you, it will be different this time."

I left that man broken, and thought what made it even more painful for him was the fact that the love she showed him was too pure and innocent for him to find elsewhere. The worst thing you can do in a relationship isn't cheating, it's not knowing the value of someone in your life. We take people for granted and if they are here now we believe that they will always be. I warned him a billion times that this might happen, but he was too stubborn to see it and too confident that no matter what happened she would never go. "She can't live without me," is what he kept saying.

"And pain will teach her to live without you," is what I kept replying.

I finished work and took the bus, hoping that Mary would at least consider talking to me. We had a good relationship, but I didn't think there was a relationship strong enough on the face of the planet that would make you forgive something so painful.

I knocked four times, but no one answered. It looked as if she wasn't in. I even tried calling her, but it went straight to voicemail. "God I hate you, Steven. I hate you so much for making me do this." I said that as I sat on the floor in front of her door, hoping that when she got back I'd be there to see her. As I was trying to make myself comfortable and prevent the cold floor from freezing my ass, I heard a voice from inside the apartment, "Zayn, I hate him too. Go away, go away, I know what you're here to say, I don't want to hear it."

Oh, God, she was there. I got up as fast as I could and said, "Mary, can I please talk to you, just for ten minutes. I swear I'm not here to change your mind or to convince you that whatever he did is forgivable. Just ten minutes, hear me out please. This is Zayn, your friend, and I honestly only care about how you feel right now."

She opened the door, didn't even look at me, and went straight back to the big chair in the corner where she sat and covered her head with all the cushions she could reach.

"Mary, Mary, get up, I need to talk to you."

"You can talk, but I'm not getting up."

"Okay, Mary, first of all, I want you to know that I hate that asshole for what he did to you. And believe me, if I was in your place I would never be able to forgive him. But, the thing is, I don't love him as much as you do, and that is my only argument, dear. Today, I saw a shade of what used to be Steven. I saw a broken, shallow human vessel with no soul floating inside. He loves you, Mary, and you were his soul and his joy in this life, even though he was stupid enough not to see it before this happened. He loves you, Mary, probably more than anyone ever will. I don't know if that word qualifies him for forgiveness, but it sure does qualify him for a chance to talk to you."

A voice coming from underneath a pile of cushions interrupted me and said, "Zayn, no one loves a person and cheats on them, no one!"

A part of me believed and agreed with that, and I wanted to tell her with all my heart that every girl deserves to be treated like she was the one and only one, but he was my friend, and I loved that idiot, so I had to keep trying as I promised him I would, "Everyone makes mistakes, Mary, but I know you love him. I know you do, and maybe, just maybe, you can find a place in your heart that can actually forgive him. I promise you that it will be different this time. I saw it in his eyes. What I saw wasn't Steven anymore. It was a shell of what he used to be. You completed him for so many years, just don't let it go now, give it a chance."

She got up so fast, pushing all the cushions away to the point where one of them hit me in the face.

I rarely saw someone with such a look of anger and sadness as she had; her eyes were swollen and red from crying for a long time. She was very pale. If I didn't know her so well, it would have been hard for me to recognize her. I guess a broken heart can make people look different. In her palm, I noticed a picture of her and Steven, squashed and wrinkled. She threw it on the floor.

"What do you know about love, huh?" she screamed at me. "What do you know about being hurt? Did someone ever cheat on you? No, not any someone, someone you love, someone you care about, someone who meant the world to you. I trusted him with all my heart, and I loved that idiot with every millimeter of my soul, but what did I get in return? You know what hurts the most? It's the fact that he thinks everything is fixable, and you being here and not him hurts even more. Well, Steven, you won't be forgiven this time I promise you that. I'm not going to lie, I know he loves me, but what I hate the most about him is the fact that every time we have a fight he's indifferent to how I feel, he doesn't care, he just thinks that because of my feelings towards him I'll always take him back. He stopped working on our relationship a long time ago, and I sure as hell know it's my goddamned fault. I hate myself because, even after this, I'm still finding excuses for him in my head, and I'm playing scenarios where he comes out innocent, just because I want him to be. I can't believe I'm pregnant with his child..."

A scary silence took over the place as that poor woman started to fall into a puddle of tears. I had never seen pain possess a human body before. With every teardrop there were a million screams of agony that came down with it. What do you say to someone like this, how can you comfort them? How can you keep your heart from breaking just from thinking about sharing that heavy burden with them? I moved closer to her and put my hand on her shoulder.

"Mary, I'm sorry, what he did is unforgivable, but just think about everything in play now, and whatever decision you are going to make I'm sure it will be the best for you. If you decide to leave him or give him another chance, I just want you to know that the human that will call you Mom wouldn't need love from any other place after he tastes what it's like to be brought up by someone like you. You have my number, please call me if you need anything."

"Thank you, Zayn, and I'm okay. Thank you for trying to fix this, I appreciate it, but I need some time alone, I hope you understand."

"Yes, of course. One last thing, dear, I know he is my friend, and I would do anything for him, but if he screwed this up for good, I'm sure that he messed up the best thing that ever happened to him, no doubt. Goodnight..."

I left her apartment carrying the weight of the world on my shoulders. What would I say to Steven? If he knew she was pregnant and she wouldn't take him back, his heart and his existence would be reduced to nothing. What if she didn't want to tell him about the pregnancy? I can't hide that from him and not for his own sake. No, but I knew what it was like not to have a father and the constant void it would leave in that poor kid's heart. I believed everything I said when I told her she wouldn't need anyone's help to give that baby all the love it deserved. But I knew the pain not having a father would leave and I was sure eventually she would feel that, so I just hoped she would find a tiny bit of mercy to forgive him with, even though I strongly doubted it.

I made it home only to notice Steven was looking out the apartment's window, waiting for me to show up. God, the truth was going to shatter him...

"What did she say, Zayn?" he asked, as I walked in the door.

"Tell me, please. Was she at least willing to talk to me? Please, Zayn, talk! What did she say?"

"She needs time, Steven. Give her some space to think, maybe then she will see that you are an idiot who might deserve a second chance. That's all I can say."

I couldn't. I couldn't drop it on him like that. I saw a glimpse of hope in his eyes that wasn't fair for me to crush. As long as there was hope he could still be the Steven I knew.

"I hope so, brother, thank you very much for everything. Here, I brought you your favorite pizza. Microwave it before you dive into it."

"Thanks, man, but I don't feel like eating now, maybe later, you can go ahead and eat."

"No, buddy, I don't feel like it."

Today was a long day, a very long, tiring day filled with sadness and tears that I hoped I could forget about. The best part was that now it was close to being over, so I hoped that tomorrow would be different. Oh crap, my phone died a while ago. I needed to charge it. Probably Mom called me a couple of times and couldn't reach me. I plugged it in the charger and laid my head on the pillow, facing the window. Steven was laying on the couch on the other side of the room. I think we both pretended to fall asleep. Silence was taking over the room until the sound of my phone vibrating broke in.

Stranger, I kind of miss talking to you. I hope you are doing well.

And just like that, the gray color that overshadowed everything went away and my heart smiled just as it did every time she talked to me. I never did drugs, but I suspect it gives you the same feeling as talking to someone whom angels would be jealous of. With her words, she was capable of taking me to another universe, another dimension that was filled with happiness, joy, and everything there revolved around the aura of grace and zeal that she blessed the people around her with. An aura that was taking from her beauty and living off her charm, giving the place her soul reached a fictitious scent that no human being like me could have enough of. Since Steven was there and he still didn't know much about her, I told him that I needed to quickly get something. I snuck myself on to the roof of the building, to my favorite spot there, the spot that I always ran to, to admire the view it had of the city, but this time I ran there wishing that I could trade the beautiful view for something more admirable.

"Hey, Farah, I hope you're not busy."

"No, Zayn, I'm not. Where have you been all day, I got a little bit worried you know."

"Sorry, if you only knew how shitty today was."

"Why, what happened?"

"I'm okay, don't worry about me. It's a long story. I don't even know where to start."

"Okay, Zayn, you sound really tired, and since you're okay I suggest you go have some rest, and let's meet tomorrow at 5 pm in Gabi's library?"

"Sounds great to be honest, can't wait to see you."

"Me too, but before you go, are you really okay, Zayn?"

"I swear I am. Especially now, after hearing your voice."

"Oh, you silly stranger, go to sleep!" she said, laughing beautifully as only she could.

"Goodnight, Princess."

"Night, Zayn."

Seven

I had never looked at the clock more than I had today. I counted every second of every hour, hoping that time would fly like an arrow heading for the demon that was the distance between her and me and kill the beast. It wasn't even 4:30 pm and no one had left yet, but I couldn't wait any longer. I wanted to go home first just so I could shower and look a bit more alive after a long day here, so I slithered my way out of there like a cobra trying to avoid a mongoose, and obviously, the mongoose here was Janice. If I was caught now it would be the end of me, but let's face it, scream, shout, humiliate or fire me, I didn't care anymore and especially when it came to meeting Farah.

I rushed home, changed my clothes, fixed my hair, and squeezed what was left from the almost completely empty cologne bottle Mom gave me for my birthday. Thinking about it, I didn't need cologne at all because the bliss of being close to her was like sitting in a garden filled with flowers, so holding one wouldn't make sense at all. I walked as fast as possible to the library, trying my best not to make her wait for me and luckily, I made it before she did. I went upstairs to the same spot we sat in the last time. Naim came and asked me if I wanted anything, so I asked that as soon as he saw Farah and me sitting down to be bring us two delicious, hot chocolates like last time.

I pulled out my phone and texted her:

Your delicious hot chocolate is waiting for you, miss.

She replied straight away:

I'm running. I'm running. I'll be there in two minutes.

I put my phone down and started to think about how lucky I was to have a person like this, and how crazy this life we were living could be; the life that could take a stranger and turn him into someone you run to when you need comfort and warmth.

I could hear her coming into the shop and saying hi to Gabi and everyone there, so I tried to pretend that I wasn't looking. As I was trying to dive into my phone, my eye caught her beautiful face coming up the stairs, and it had a smile that melted my heart, so I just kept admiring what was in front of me.

"Sorry for being late, Zayn, how are you?"

"I'm upset because you're late. No, I'm more than upset."

"Don't be silly, it was only five minutes." she said, laughing.

"No, I'm hurt and the only way I can forget about it is if you stay with me longer than you were planning to."

She laughed and said, "And I will happily do so, Mister, just so you aren't mad with me."

She sat next to me as we started talking about everything, and she went through my worries and problems like I go through books page by page, slowly and attentively trying not to miss any lines. I told her about Steven and his story, and a tear rolled from her eye as soon as she heard that Mary was bearing his child. She told me about the problems she was facing with courses, studies, and life. Through all the mess we were talking about and the dilemmas we were uncovering, I felt that no one would ever get me as much as this girl did. I never felt this safe around anyone before and I took a moment when she was taking a sip of her drink to pause everything and just admire the fact that, for some reason, I did something so right in my life to deserve someone like this heavenly creature in front of me.

"Farah, I have never enjoyed anyone's company more than I do yours."

"Zayn, I never enjoyed drinking hot chocolate next to anyone as much as I do with you by my side. I feel like taking a walk, do you want to come with me?"

"Great idea, let's go."

We left the bookshop and started roaming around our sad city, our broken city. There was this layer of sadness that covered everything since the riots started, and the fear that overcame the people was now so obvious even though everyone was trying to act brave in front of each other. They were trying to scream freedom and to catch the train of civilization bringing democracy to our small world, but for some reason, the capital didn't see it that way, and it tried in every way possible to shut the voices of liberty down. Uncle Jamal said that we were in for a showdown in the near future.

Farah and I walked as if we didn't care about any of that, and our laughter was heard from every corner of the almost empty road. We stopped in front of every shop whose owner was brave enough to keep it open and looked through the windows, picking out things we wished we could buy in the future. We made it past a musical instrument shop where we decided that it was a good idea to go in and play a little bit with the pianos and the guitars. We went in and started to produce weird noises with everything we touched, laughing so hard trying not to let the owner throw us out, and made it to an amazing piano that was in the center of the shop.

"All my life I wished I could learn to play the piano." I said, looking at her walking towards it.

"Well, I can teach you if you want."

"Excuse me, miss, I said play the piano, not make noises with it."

"Oh, we all have secrets, Zayn."

She sat in front of the piano, and as soon as her fingers started touching the keys, my jaw dropped and I couldn't believe what I was hearing. She actually played the piano. She gave me this cute smirk and said, "This song is for you, stranger."

Every time her fingers touched those notes I felt its vibrations deep inside my heart. The song was familiar. I didn't know where I had heard it before, but my brain could remember it, and my eyes couldn't stop cherishing that moment. To sum it all up, I couldn't focus on anything. I kept staring at how she moved. I was mesmerized at how charmingly she was slowly moving her head, following the rhythm and making her hair fall on her shoulders, looking as beautiful as ever. The melody was becoming increasingly familiar, until she hit one note, and with it tears started to make their way down my cheeks. I recognized the song. It was what my father used to play for me when I was a naughty kid who needed to go to bed but refused to until he played that tune. It took me back to when life still held some meaning for me, and just like that, I was visiting that happy place I always went to when I needed comfort. She took my hand and flew with it in the air towards the memory of my Superman that I held up there, guarded by all the happy memories I ever felt. She looked at me and was more than surprised to see me tear up, so she stopped and tried to reach for my hand that was wiping the tears off my face.

"No, please don't, please keep going."

"But, Zayn, why?"

"Farah, I have a history with that instrumental you were playing, I haven't listened to it in more than fifteen years, so please…"

She started playing again, and this time I saw it clearly in front of me. I saw my father wearing his blue jacket, playing the piano with my mom standing next to him telling me to go to bed, and me holding on to him screaming, "Mom, please just one more, one more song, Mom, please. I want him to teach me to play so I become as good as him."

He would always stand up for his little boy and said, "If I teach you, Son, you will be better than me, there is no doubt." Only my eyes found a way to express what I felt as they poured, watching Farah playing the piano. This moment had alleviated my soul, so I put my hand on her shoulder and said, "Thank you, Farah, you will never know what this means to me."

She stopped and looked at me, and I saw her face covered with tears, the sad look she had in her eyes and the red color that her tiny nose took.

"I'm sorry, Zayn, I'm sorry that someone like you suffered that much, if only life was fair people like you wouldn't…"

"Shh." I used my fingers to seal her lips together, looked at her, and just felt guilty for making her cry. I sat next to her as she held my hand in hers, and her head found its way on to my shoulder, and for the first time in years, I felt what it was like to have someone who shares your sadness and actually cares for you. Her hand fitted into mine just like it was the last piece of the puzzle and now that it was in its place, everything made sense, and I was able to admire the whole picture. And there was no picture more beautiful than her holding me close. Now I believed in fate, as it led me to this miracle sitting next to me.

"Farah, I think we didn't meet out of pure luck. I think that God sent you my way just to prove to me that there are still miracles in this world, and that there is still hope for sad, lonely people like me to be happy."

She tried to wipe her tears away, and looked at me with the prettiest smile ever.

"And I think you came into my life as a stranger hiding behind a curtain, and as soon as I took a peek behind the drapery I saw the purest heart anyone could ever have decorated with the cutest smile I have ever seen. I saw someone who got me from day one. Zayn, knowing you didn't feel like knowing a person for the first time, it felt like catching up with my best friend. No, it felt like getting my soulmate back into my life."

Eight

Joy is what I call my life now, or maybe, to be more accurate, a bundle of joy is what I feel every day with that girl diving deeper and deeper in my heart. With all the elation I was in, I couldn't ignore what was going on around me anymore. The city was crippled now, and almost everything went downhill in the last couple of days. The people were now screaming louder with their search for freedom. Almost every day a demonstration occurred. It wasn't safe to go out after a protest took place because the police would hunt you down. As soon as you stepped foot in the street you were automatically considered to be one of the people inciting the riots and causing the civil unrest, so every day they sent us home from work early. I couldn't complain to be honest, even though they were cutting down our salaries due to the lack of business and production issues that were caused by the protests. I didn't care as I used that time to see Farah. We met almost every day and talked and drew what I consider to be the happiest moments of my life with majestic brushes.

Today was no different when it came to work. I left early and ran home because I had something very important to plan. Today was the day God decided to bless this world with one of the most beautiful creations he ever created. It was her birthday. I tried playing it very cool, doing my best not to make her feel anything and even went to the extent of telling her that I had plans today with another friend and that I wasn't free to see her. The hardest part of this beautiful day was figuring out what gift would be worthy enough to be hers. I didn't know what to get her. I mean, the gift should be a symbol of how important she was to me, so maybe I should throw a rope and try to bring down the moon to her feet, just so it knows that no matter how bright it shines it will never be as beautiful as her. Or maybe I should climb a ladder all the way up to the sky, collect every star there is, and just put them around her to make her realize that she was the most elegant star in any celestial sphere that ever existed. But for now, I'd settle for the things that I could actually reach and had a couple of ideas to choose from.

Alongside the lessons in happiness I was learning from my relationship with Farah, I was also learning about heartbreaks and disappointments from Steven and Mary. She took the decision that she wanted nothing to do with Steven, even though I tried everything in my power to make her at least tell him that she was pregnant and see where they could go from there. But their relationship was broken beyond repair in her opinion, and she even made me swear not to tell him anything. To her, what he did was unforgivable, and no matter how much she tried to forget, that picture of him with someone else would end up haunting her for the rest of her life. I honestly couldn't argue that a day would come when I'd tell him everything and he would hate me for keeping this secret from him, but he will understand, I'm sure.

It had been a long time since I had swung by Uncle Jamal's

café so I decided today might be a good day to listen to the old man's stories and him analyzing every small detail of the news they cover on TV. The café was next to the flower shop, and I planned to get a bouquet for Farah on my way back.

"Hey, Uncle Jamal, how are you today?"

"Oh, Zayn, long time no see, how are you, Son?"

"Yeah, I missed you guys. I missed that delicious coffee you make."

"One special coffee heading your way, Son, and sit here, I need to talk to you."

I sat down in my usual spot looking around at what used to be the busiest place in this neighborhood. It was almost empty, and this was the first time I ever saw it this way. It was the most famous coffee house here. Everyone knew "Café el Hayat" as Uncle Jamal named it. Everyone knew each other, they used to sit, talk, laugh, and joke about with each other, and no one would leave that place angry. That was Uncle Jamal's philosophy behind naming the place "Hayat" – it meant life. He felt that the kind of relationship people built out of laughter and jokes was the one that endured the test of time and that was how life should be lived.

"You look surprised that the place is empty!" said Uncle Jamal, pouring the coffee in a cup.

"Yeah, I've never seen it this way."

"It's been like this for more than a month. People fear coming here. They are afraid that the police will come and arrest everyone, thinking that we are planning something here. If they even think that you might be saying the word 'protest' in your head you will be arrested automatically, no question."

"Yeah, I heard people talk about their relatives disappearing just like that, and later they discovered that they were held in some prison or police station, can you believe that?"

"Yes, I can," he said, as he sat next to me.

"Son, do you still work at that company? Because I heard a lot of the foreign companies are closing down."

"Yes, I still do, but we only work from eight to twelve noon every day. The company is closing down by the end of the month, and they are moving everything to Europe. I think, some of the hot shot employees are attached to it and they are moving as well."

"Oh, are you going?"

I laughed and said to myself, *yes, they are probably going to take the most useless guy there with them.*

"No, Uncle, I'm not that important there."

"Ah, and what are you planning to do after your job there is over?"

"I haven't thought about that, Uncle. I don't know. Maybe I'll go back to the capital and stay with my mom for a couple of days, and then figure it out from there."

"That might be a good thing to do, Zayn, it's not safe here anymore, and word is spreading about some people forming a militia. An armed militia, Zayn, and they are planning to force the president to step down. From what I know, he will never bow down to them. And I assure you, we are the ones who are going to suffer. Normal people like you who have nothing to do with any of this are going to suffer. Leave as soon as you can, the capital might be a very good choice."

"And what about you, Uncle, when are you leaving?"

He looked at me as if I had told the world's least funny joke, and said, "Where will I go, Son? I lived all my life here. All the good moments I ever lived were between these walls and down that street. I never traveled anywhere, and I'm not going to leave everything I worked for all my life out of fear. Let them arrest me or even worse, let them kill me. I would die here with a smile on my face knowing that the grave that's going to hold my body down is made from familiar soil, soil that watched me grow old day by day. At least it won't be that lonely down there."

I have never seen or heard him talk like this. It was as if Uncle Jamal was scared, but at the same time, he was too brave to admit it.

"Uncle!" I said, "Hopefully, none of that will happen. You know, as they say, it's always darkest before dawn, have faith, we will be all right."

"Yeah, I'm sure we will. Please, Zayn, if you need anything I'm always here, okay, Son?"

"Thank you so much, Uncle, you are one of the very few people who made me fall in love with this city. I have to go now, see you soon."

"Take good care of yourself, Son, and before you leave, come and say goodbye."

"I will, Uncle, have a lovely day."

"As if that's possible," he yelled at me as I walked away.

I left the café and crossed the street to the flower shop, trying not to think about what Uncle Jamal just said. Leaving this city and going back home wasn't that bad an idea to be honest. When I thought about leaving, my heart just dropped and it felt as if every part of my soul hated the idea, and the reason was if I had to leave it meant I had to let go of the only thing I cared about, Farah. I wasn't capable of thinking about doing that, let alone actually leaving. I realized I was addicted now, addicted to the most powerful drug ever created, and if

I stopped using it now, my body, my soul, and my heart would never be the same. Can you tell anything about someone from their favorite color of flower? Farah loved white flowers and I don't think it would have made sense if she loved any other color. I mean, white is the color of purity, perfection, and completion. It's the color that offers an inner cleansing and purifying of your thoughts. It is peace and comfort and helps alleviate emotional upsets. *Zayn, isn't she all of that to you?*

We were set to meet in the afternoon, and I was hoping that we could go to the park that was very close to her place, and until now it was considered to be part of the safe areas in the city. We thought it was a place where we could sit and admire the nature, the view, the trees, the plants, and birds. Well, she could admire that, I'd probably be admiring her.

I was home getting myself ready when my phone rang. It was Farah

"Hey, dear, what's up?"

"Hey, Zayn, not much to be honest, how are you?"

"I'm okay, just getting myself ready for later, we can meet now if you want."

"About that, I don't think I can make it to be honest. As you know, my parents aren't here, and my little sister is sick, and I don't think I can leave her alone."

"Oh, I see, I hope she gets better soon, take good care of her. We can meet some other time, don't worry."

"Don't be mad with me, okay, Zayn. You know I want to see you, right?"

"I'm not mad, Farah. Well, you're probably not in the mood to cook anything, so as compensation for not meeting me, can I bring you pizza later?"

"Oh, my God, you're so sweet, but I'm the one canceling.

I'm the one who should be making up for it, not you." she said, laughing.

"Just say yes, please."

"Okay, I'll be waiting. I'm not excited about seeing you by the way. I'm only interested in eating the pizza you bring."

I burst out laughing.

"Oh, really, no pizza then, I'll bring you a salad."

"No. I take it back. I miss you so much, please come see me pizza man/soulmate."

"I will. I'll see you in a bit."

As I hung up, I had one question on my mind, from where would I be able to buy pizza right now? Every pizza place was closed. I realized I might have put myself in big, big trouble. I texted Steven to see if he could help me out and ran to this restaurant next to my building, hoping and praying that it was still open. Apparently, the one time she asked something from me I'm not going to be able to get it for her. That dumbass, Steven, replied, 'I have last week's pizza. If you want you can come get it.' I didn't even respond to him and kept running. God, please don't make me disappoint her, "Isn't that Madame Jamila?" I said to myself.

"Hey, Madame, how are you? Do you know if that restaurant down the street is still open?"

"Hey, Zayn, why are you running, are you that hungry?" she asked, laughing.

Oh, my God, you people with your jokes right when I don't need them, I said to myself.

"No Zayn, I was just there, and it's closed. I think people broke in the place and stole equipment and things from there, you know how it is now, no one is safe."

"Yeah, bad things keep happening to us, Madame, anyway,

catch you later. I have to go, stay safe okay."

I was walking back home disappointed when I had the greatest idea in the history of ideas. Why don't I make the pizza? I made it before and I'd watched millions of videos on how to make it, so YouTube would make me a good enough Italian chef. I thought I'd make it myself and she would either love me for it or never speak to me again, probably because she might die after I poisoned her. Oh, God, I hope I don't poison her. Zayn, *stop freaking out,* I said to myself, *it's easy, you can do this.*

I ran to the supermarket and thanked God when I saw it open. I grabbed everything I needed and went back home. Trying to remember the recipe was the hardest part, and we didn't have internet anymore so I couldn't look it up online. The government was so scared about the people organizing marches through Facebook that they had a breakthrough idea "disconnect the whole country from the internet. That way they won't be able to plan anything". But what about the people who just want to make pizza, huh? I didn't have a choice; I was going to have to work with what I had. I just hoped it came out from the oven as close as possible to a pizza.

It was almost seven pm and the thing was nearly ready, so I texted Farah *Are you ready for the world's most delicious pizza ever?* She replied within seconds, *Hell, yeah I am, we are starving here.* I tasted it, and to be honest, it wasn't that bad, I was kind of proud of myself, so I wrote, *Be right there.* I cut everything into slices and put it in a plastic container. I wore my coat, grabbed the flower bouquet and her gift, and started my small adventure to Farah's house.

I'm saying adventure because it was late now and the

police were patrolling every road leading up to her house, and we were living in a dusk to dawn curfew. So, if they saw me, they were probably going to arrest me. I didn't know where I got the courage, but I was determined to get there in time. Farah kept calling me, after hearing the police sirens she was definitely scared that something bad might happen to me. Sorry, dear soulmate, but I'm not going to pick up just so you tell me I don't have to come. I was almost there when I suddenly heard the police car pull up behind me and a police officer talking through the speaker, "Freeze right there. You are breaking the law. Stop, stop right there!"

I freaked out and started running like a maniac, "Open the door, the police are chasing me," I screamed down the phone as I ran faster, the flash of white as every flower in the bouquet flew somewhere. The pizza probably looked like it tasted now after being bounced around by all the running.

I could see Farah standing next to the door, telling me to run faster, and could hear the police car making a turn my way. I could barely move my feet anymore, but I kept pushing until I made it through the door and fell to the ground out of breath, looking a mess.

"Close the do... close the door," I mumbled.

"Oh, God, Zayn, what if they had caught you? What if something happened to you over pizza that I made you get for me? I called like a million times to tell you that you shouldn't come. I forgot about the curfew. Do you want me to live feeling guilty forever?"

"Wait ... wait a second before we go anywhere, I didn't come here for the pizza alone. I'm sorry, Farah, they ruined this for me. Here, I know this doesn't look like a bouquet of flowers anymore, but the main reason I came here was to wish you a happy birthday. I didn't want you to spend it alone as if it was a normal day. No, twenty-two years ago God blessed the world with you, and that shouldn't go unnoticed. I'm sorry, there were sixteen flowers here, one for each week we have been in each other's lives, but there's only one left I think. I'm sorry, I wanted to make it special for you, but I ruined it like I always do. I'm sorry."

A moment of silence took us both into a journey of gazing into each other's eyes. She stared at me with that look of fondness, tears in her eyes, but no words in her mouth, as she sat on the ground with me.

"You are happiness to me, Zayn. I'm so choked I don't even know what to say anymore. 'Thank you' doesn't even come close. I have never had such a pleasant surprise. I don't think my heart will ever beat as fast as it's doing right now. Zayn, I don't need sixteen flowers. Zayn, I don't even need one. I have you."

She took the flower out of the bouquet and held it close to her chest.

"And it's white, my favorite color. How did you know?"

I laughed as I said, "Your favorite color might be purple, you favorite chocolate is dark chocolate, and you love white flowers."

"I don't know what I have done in my life to deserve someone special like you. You keep brightening my soul. Get up, Zayn, get up."

I stood as she threw herself into my arms, her head finding its way onto my chest right above my heart, and I bet she heard it beating louder than those police sirens outside. For the time I was hugging her I felt complete. I felt safe as I whispered, "I don't want to let go..."

"Me, neither."

We made our way into the living room, and she told me to put the pizza in the kitchen and come upstairs to her little sister's bedroom. Her poor little sister was sick with the flu, and could barely get out of bed.

"Farah, when are your parents coming back? Are they still in Italy?"

"Yes, they are still there. Dad finished work about two weeks ago, and they are supposed to be here now but due to the airports closing down and the limited number of flights the government is allowing they couldn't make it back yet. I'm scared, Zayn, I really am. I didn't want to tell you this, but I'm terrified. I also don't want to go to my grandparents' house. To be honest, it's far away, depressing, and if I go, I'm not going to be able to see you for God knows how long."

"It's okay, don't go anywhere, I'm here. I won't leave you alone and I'll die before I let anything happen to you. Tell me, did you check Jasmine's temperature?"

"Yes, I did and thank God it went down. In the morning, I took her to our neighbor, the doctor I told you about, and he gave me pills and syrup for her cough and it looks as if they have started working."

"Okay, I'm going to go microwave that pizza, you're probably starving. I'll be right back."

For some weird reason, and after all that running I did, the pizza still looked quite all right. I chose the best slices I could find and put them on a plate, microwaved the whole thing, looked at it while it was turning in the microwave, and said a little prayer hoping that she would like it.

"Zayn, is everything all right, do you need some help?"

"No, I'm coming up, get ready for the world's most

delicious pizza."

"Hurry up then, bring the ketchup bottle with you…"

"Really, Farah, ketchup with pizza?"

"Don't ask, just bring it."

Everything was special about that girl, even the fact that she liked ketchup and ate it with almost everything. I put the plate and the bottle on the cute desk Jasmine had in her room and said, "Farah, wake Jasmine up, she needs to eat something."

"I did wake her up, she keeps on saying no."

"Okay, step away from her and let me try."

"Oh, okay, Mister-I-Can-Convince-An-Eleven-Year-Old-With-Anything, the stage is all yours."

"Jasmine… Jasmine, Sweetie, you need to wake up. I know you can hear me, come on, wake up. I promise you if you do when you get better I'll take you somewhere really nice and get you your favorite ice cream and we can play there all day. Your favorite is strawberry ricotta isn't it?"

A sweet, tired voice came from underneath the covers and said, "I'm only waking up because of the ice cream you just promised me, and because Farah talks about you all the time and I want to finally meet you."

I was so excited and turned around to see Farah actually even more surprised, looking at me with that 'don't you even dare to show off look'. The little angel sat on her bed and looked like a tiny butterfly looking for a place to rest on.

"Here you go, just a couple of bites and then we can go back to sleep, I know you like pizza, and this is not just a pizza, this is my pizza. I made it myself."

Farah tapped me on the shoulder.

"Did you actually make the pizza?"

"Well, yeah. It's not a big deal. You said you wanted pizza, and all the places were closed, so I decided to make it myself. Don't worry, it tastes good. Probably..." I laughed, trying to hide my worry.

"Yeah, I said I wanted pizza but I didn't want you to go to all the trouble of making it for me."

"Number one, it's your birthday. So, you're allowed to ask for the Moon and if you did, I'd climb up there and bring it down to your feet. Number two, what kind of soulmate would I be if you ask something of me and I don't do it for you? I think that's punishable by the soulmate police. Number three, I know it's your favorite food. I just hope you like my version of it."

"Well, Farah said that you are the sweetest man on Earth, now I understand why," Jasmine said with a smile on her face.

"Oh, stop it. I did nothing, Jasmine. The reason I came here was to see you. It had nothing to do with Farah." I whispered to her. She laughed and started eating her slice of pizza while I took one and gave it to Farah, praying to God that she would also like it.

"Go ahead, take a bite, tell me what you think."

"I can't believe you did this, Zayn, I just can't."

"Forget about believing, it's time to start eating."

I sat on the chair facing the bed and watched Farah gently put her little sister back to sleep after she finished her slice. A feeling rushed to the deepest part of my fast-beating heart, a feeling of bravery and courage. Not the courage that would make you face the world's scariest monsters, but the courage that makes you not mind the world ending right this second, as long as the reflection of that girl is painted on your cornea and her presence is filling you heart with every good feeling you ever wished to encounter. I fell even deeper into the sea of elegance as she read a bedtime story to Jasmine. Before the little girl closed her eyes she looked at me and said, "It was nice to meet you, Zayn. I really like you. You make my sister happy, and that means you make me happy."

"You make me happy as well Sweetie, and I'm going to keep my word. After you are well I will take you out. Just you and me. And I promise we're going to have so much fun."

"Thank you so much, goodnight."

"Goodnight."

Farah sat next to me and whispered, "I can't believe how you turned this night upside down. I was having such a crappy day and was scared about Jasmine being sick, but you coming here and going to all that trouble just to be here with me and to wish me a happy birthday is something I'll never forget, Zayn. Well, everything you do is unforgettable, but this is…"

"Stop, please stop. I'm your best friend, Farah, your best friend and your soulmate. You don't have to thank me when I do something like this. In fact, you have to get angry with me if I do any less. I want to make another pinkie promise deal with you. As long as there is air coming out of our lungs, and as long as our eyes still see this sad little world we live in, promise me that we will be in each other's lives no matter what. Promise me that we will never give up on this relationship. Promise me if I fall you will pick me up. And I promise you, if one day you break your wings I'll give you mine to fly with. I honestly can't imagine my life without you, and I'll do anything to put a smile on that beautiful face of yours."

"You're the best birthday gift I ever had and…"

"Will you guys shut up. I'm trying to sleep in here." Jasmine yelled while coughing from underneath her covers.

We both burst out laughing, and I left the room as Farah kissed her sister and told her to call for her if she needed anything.

"We'll be in my room, Sweetie, goodnight."

We sat next to the window, and nothing was more beautiful than the moonlight's reflection on the prettiest face I had ever seen. I made her close her eyes, reached down to my pocket, and grabbed the gift I had for her.

"No, don't open your eyes yet, this needs an introduction."

"Oh, my God, Zayn. Why…"

"Farah, don't talk, just listen. I wrote you a letter that was meant to go with the bouquet. The flowers didn't survive my run here, but at least the letter did. I wrote this down because I knew if I tried saying these things face to face looking at you I'd probably stumble and forget how to speak. Just listen to me, because when you look through me with those piercing, beautiful eyes of yours, I can only do one thing, and that's drown in the ocean of memories and grace I see in yours…

"Dear Farah

I have known sadness, fear, and loss for as long as I can remember. Ever since my father died, life has been like an old TV for me; black and white with a miserable, static sound with no decent picture coming through its screen. And I grew used to it, until I saw you that day in the bus.

I don't know what it is, and to this day, I can't explain it. You were a stranger to me, but when I look at you every fiber in my body is like, "There she is". It is an overwhelming feeling of joy, and it feels as if I'm on the waiting list for an organ transplant, a set of lungs, or maybe a heart.

Then the phone call came in, 'we are ready for you, Zayn,

come and let us bring you back to life.' And to this day that's exactly what you are to me, a ride back from the lost and lonely land I was trapped in. Today is your birthday. Today is the day God blessed this world with your presence, twenty-two years ago, and I can't thank him enough for that. Having you in my life is a true testament that miracles still exist and that God might have listened to my prayers asking him to pull me out of that dark tunnel I was living in. I got you something, something that doesn't even come close to what you deserve. I just hope you like it and that it will be with you forever.

Your Soulmate"

I looked at her only to see that her eyes were filled with tears and her nose was that cute, raspberry color.

"Your gift. I hope you like it."

The gift was a bracelet that I had custom-made for her. It was one of the classiest things I had ever seen. It had three tiny hearts dangling from it. On the first one, I had them engrave the date of the first time I saw her. On the second one, there was a quote that she absolutely loved, "Along with every hardship is relief", which translated how she looked at the world. I had known her for a while now, and almost every time I saw her, no matter the pain or the problems she was going through, a beautiful smile was always decorating her hope-filled face. She has faith that the future is only hiding good things for us. On the third heart there was another quote, but I wanted that one to be a constant reminder of how much she means to me. I wrote, "When I'm with you I feel safe from the things that hurt me inside". I gave her the bracelet knowing that whatever message I leave her with and no matter how valuable the material it's made from, it won't be enough to describe how much she means to me.

She read and saw all of that, and the few teardrops turned into a waterfall of diamonds that I felt on my cheek as she hugged me so tight that I felt our souls mixing together, as if they weren't already mixed…

"Zayn, you are my everything. I don't even know what else to say, don't you ever leave me!"

"Leave you. I'd rather die a million deaths before I do. I'll always be with you. We are soulmates, remember. It was written in the stars for our souls to meet. How could our bodies deny that and let go of each other?"

We created a safe haven in each other's arms, ignoring the police sirens, the explosions we heard from afar, and the bullets being shot frequently to remind us that our world was crumbling into the unknown that we were probably going to get lost in. But we chose to ignore that and focus on the fact that, as long as our souls were holding each other tightly, everything was going to be all right.

"Zayn, what do you think is happening outside?"

"I spoke with Uncle Jamal today and he said there is an armed militia preparing itself to take over the country and, of course, take down the president."

"Oh, my God, and what are we going to do?"

"I guess we are going to wait it out, what choice do we have? It's not safe for us to go anywhere except maybe the capital. I'm going to try and figure out how we can go there. You see…"

"We?" she said, laughing.

"Yes. We. What, did you think I was going to leave you and that sister of yours here? Mom is really worried about me and is trying to see if she can send my stepdad here to pick me up. Of course, when he comes you're going with me as well. Otherwise, I'm obviously not leaving, because even when your parents arrive their plane will land at the airport in the capital, so it will be easier for you to meet them!"

"But, Zayn, your mom doesn't even…"

"Doesn't even know about you? Don't you think she noticed that her son was happier than he ever was and asked him why, and he said he'd met his soulmate? You're going with me, Farah, please don't argue. I'm going to keep you guys safe until your parents come back. If you say no one more time I'll go right now and you'll probably never see me again!"

"Don't you ever say that!" she shouted at me while gently laying her head on my shoulder. "Where have you been all my life, soulmate, where have you been?"

"I was learning how hard, lonely, and sad life was before you. Simple."

"You are my everything!"

"Farah!" Jasmine screamed from her room, terrified by the explosions that were getting closer each time.

"I'm coming, Sweetie. I'm here."

We tried to calm her down, and this time she asked us to stay with her and not leave. The stars above us witnessed the beautiful melody our laughter composed, but they also witnessed what was going on outside, and the dark hole the explosions were pushing our little haven into.

Nine

The sunlight gently woke me. I opened my eyes only to realize that I had slept sitting down, facing the window, and Farah had used my shoulder as a pillow. It was only 6:45 am, but I was worried and intrigued to go outside to see what had happened last night. It was the first time ever we heard bullets and explosions that close. Although it sounded quiet outside, I knew that behind the silence hid a new chapter of our life.

"Farah, wake up." I whispered in her ear.

"What time is it?"

"Morning, dear, it's 6:48, did you sleep well?"

"If by 'well' you mean every bone in my back hurts, then yes, I slept very well. Morning."

"Oh, sorry to hear that. Why don't you go check on Jasmine, and then you can go back to sleep, this time in your comfortable bed."

"That is the best thing you've said since I've known you, Zayn. It sounds quiet outside; do you think whatever happened is over now?"

"Who knows. I'm going to my apartment, and I'll ask around the neighborhood and see what shape last night left our city in."

"It's not safe, are you crazy? You're not going anywhere. I'm scared, and you're the only one I can trust here. Zayn, can you just stay here? Forget about going anywhere, please. I mean we can keep each other company. I think that would be best. Please, Zayn, you can sleep in my bed, and I'll sleep with Jasmine."

"You would do that for me? You would give me your bed to sleep in? I think that's the sweetest thing anyone has ever done for me." I said that with a sarcastic smirk on my face knowing how much she loved her bed.

"Actually, come to think about it, you can sleep in Jasmine's bed, my bed is too precious for me to give away. Sorry, soulmate."

"Oh, really," I said, laughing. "Not even for me?"

"Just get your things and come back. I'm going to wake Jasmine to see if she feels any better then I'll call my parents and see how they are doing. Don't take too long, okay, and promise that you'll be safe."

"I promise, don't you worry, Farah."

"No, pinkie promise."

"You're so funny, girl, I swear. Here you go."

We pinkie promised and I guaranteed for the millionth time that I wouldn't be gone for long and I'd be back soon so we could have breakfast together. I also kissed Jasmine goodbye and she filled my heart with joy when I saw her smiling and feeling a bit better.

It was really cold and gloomy outside, and what made it even drearier was the fog that took over the place. I couldn't see farther than a couple of meters ahead. The sadness I felt really got to me as fear found its way into my heart. It was dead silent almost everywhere. I could hear cars on the highway, which wasn't far away, and that was it. The streets were empty. No stores, bakeries, or no cafés were open. I thought the only place that might still have a brave owner to defy this fear was Uncle Jamal's café. It wasn't far, and he normally opened around this time, so I decided to go and talk to him. But first I needed to call my mom to see how she was doing and ask when her husband would be able to come and get us out of here. I hadn't realized that my phone had died. Oh, God, she probably called me last night a billion times and got more than worried when I didn't reply. She was going to kill me for putting her through all of that, but I needed to find a way to call her.

On my way to Uncle Jamal's café, I passed what used to be a police station. I guessed it was the first line of the new chapter that this day brought, and it wasn't looking good. I was so choked that what used to be a police station was just a pile of dust now. There wasn't even a wall standing in the place. There were no police officers, police cars, nothing, just smoke and rubble everywhere. What or who did this? Normally, the police were the ones breaking people's doors down and arresting whomever they wanted, and no one dared to say anything. I needed answers before I started freaking out. Thank goodness I could see Uncles Jamal's café was open so he would probably help me make sense of all this.

"Uncle, are you there?"

"One second, I'll be right there."

"It's me, Zayn. Take your time, Uncle."

He appeared from behind the counter carrying a box of coal, which people use to light and smoke the hookah. What was special about this man was that nothing could shake him, no matter what happened. I could see in his eyes that there wasn't an ounce of worry or fear. I wished I had been as strong as him last night. With every explosion, I heard my heart jump from its place and I kept praying with all my heart that God would keep my angel safe. Farah was holding on to me, trying to seek comfort in my arms, but in fact, it was the complete opposite. I didn't know what would have happened to me if I had been alone through all of it.

"Zayn, what are you doing here this early?"

"Didn't you hear what happened last night, Uncle? I came looking for answers."

"Yes, of course, I have the answer. It's the same as yesterday's answer. Leave, Son. Leave as soon as you can, while you still can. What you heard yesterday was the sound of the birds of hell flapping their wings above our neighborhood. The militia I told you about were the ones responsible for it. They have a huge arsenal of weapons that only God knows where it came from. And as you can see, they successfully kicked the police out of the city, and we can now say that our lives belong to them. I doubt the capital and military will react to this. From what I saw yesterday, and from what I heard, they are no match for these rebels."

I stood there, not knowing what to say or how to react to what he was saying.

"But who are these people?"

"I chose not to speak about the dark side of all of this the last time you asked me and hoped it would be solved. I honestly didn't expect them to be tactical and get here this fast. Fear like this cripples people, Zayn, and I didn't want you to be its victim. Here's the truth, Son. They claim to be soldiers of God and they infiltrated our small villages on the outskirts, where they planted the seed of violence and corrupted values in the easily impressionable youth. Do you know Umailim? It's the first place this plague infected because it's very close to the border and where they come from. My wife was born and raised there, and now all her family are trapped inside what was a beautiful city like ours. Zayn, these people are the definition of destruction. They have their own rules, laws, and punishments. They look at themselves as true liberators, taking us from the deep, hellish well of sin into the light of righteousness. If you choose a different path from the one they set for you, it is considered defiance and a menace to their faith and beliefs. With that excuse in their hands, my son, they have the right to end your life. I'm sorry, I know this is distressing to hear, but I told you the sad truth that we will face soon, just so you'll be ready."

I couldn't actually process what he was saying. Was I living a lie, or had my stupidity made me live in the dark? I lived in my own bubble that I created and safely guided to isolate me from what was going on outside my circle of interest. This wasn't a day and night thing. *How could I not see this coming? What should I do now?* I asked myself.

"Uncle, can I use your phone, please, I need to call my mom."

"Of course."

I dialed her number, praying that she was okay.

"Mom, hello, it's me, did I wake you up?"

"Zayn! Where the hell have you been?" She screamed at me as I heard her burst into tears. "Why didn't you answer, you stupid idiot? I called you a million times last night, and it kept going straight to voicemail. Why would you do that to me? Where are you now, are you okay? Did anything bad happen close to where you live?"

"Mom, I'm sorry, I swear I didn't mean to upset you, please forgive me. My phone died and I didn't notice until now. I'm sorry, please don't be mad with me. I'm okay now. I'm calling you from Uncle Jamal's phone. You remember, I told you about him before."

"I'm not mad. I'm just out of this world worried, Son. I was watching the news yesterday. I didn't sleep, those animals are taking over the country, Zayn. I was planning to…"

"Mom, I'm scared," I said, as I tried not to cry in front of this statue of bravery called Jamal. "I don't know what to do, Mom. This happened so fast, and no one expected it to be like this. Am I trapped here?"

Uncle Jamal gently tapped me on the back and whispered, "Stay strong, for your mom." I hadn't realized that I was already crying and panicking.

"Zayn, they said in the news yesterday that these people are trying to isolate the places they control from the rest of the country. I want you to stay strong, Son. I'm sorry I'm not there with you right now, but I'm coming with Bassem to get you out of there. It doesn't matter if I have to walk there, just stay safe until I do."

"Mom, Mom, it's too dangerous for you to come. I swear, if anything happens to you or your husband because of me it will be worse than a million painful deaths by these people. I would never be able to live with myself. Mom, I'll be okay. We just have to wait and see. Maybe I'll be able to get out of here on my own. It would be easier than you coming all the way here."

"No, Zayn, this isn't a request, I'm coming to get my son out of there."

We both started crying. Mom wasn't able to keep talking

any more, and I didn't find words to comfort her with. I needed her, but I didn't know how to hide that from her, so I just gave in to the tears that I think spoke louder than the false confidence I was wearing. I looked at Uncle Jamal, only to see tears in his eyes as well. The eyes that withstood fear and showed bravery last night bowed down in front the sadness the distance between my mom and I caused. As soon as he saw me looking, he turned his face and tried to wipe the tears. Clearly, for a strong man like him, crying is embarrassing.

Mom held herself together as she finished, "I love you more than life itself, and more than this distance between us. I love you, Son. You are my one and only, and I'm coming to get you. What am I without you, Zayn? Please stay safe until I see you. Recharge your phone and I'll be in touch. I'm going to check with Karim if we can come today."

"I will, Mom. Don't worry, please. I'll call you later, I promise. I love you, Mom."

"Take care of yourself, Son. I love you more."

I gave Uncle Jamal's phone back and stood there with tears in my eyes, not knowing what to do or what to say. Everything went even darker in my head, and the scary fact that hit me right there and then was that maybe this is the last time I'll ever speak to my mom!

If death is what's waiting for me then I accept it and whatever comes with it, but God protect my mom, please. I couldn't live if anything happened to her, God. Please, you took my dad away from me and I lived all my life with a piece of my heart missing, just don't hurt the other piece. Please.

"Zayn! Zayn, where did you go?"

"Yes, Uncle, what?"

"I was talking to you and then I realized that you weren't

even listening. It's okay, Son, your mom will be okay. You need to stay strong. I'm here for you. You have my number, and I'll see what I can do about arranging a way for you to get out of here, so don't worry."

"Thank you, Uncle. You have no idea how grateful I am for having you in my life. I have to go now. I'll catch up with you later."

"Zayn, remember what used to be your safe neighborhood is a war zone now, just be prepared for anything."

So, this was what being lost felt like. As I walked home, I kept staring left and right at the emptiness of the void that was taking over. I had hated my job for as long as I could remember, and I hated the fact that my future wasn't planned as I wanted it to be. I thought that was what being lost must be like. But this had opened my eyes to things far bigger than that. I knew these roads I was walking on. I knew the people who lived here, and I was used to the birds chattering in the trees, but I felt as if my soul had left my body.

I was feeling as if the reality that was being forced upon us was slowly suffocating me and my very soul. I had to quickly get home and then back to the only thing that was keeping me together. Farah. At least with her I could feel somewhat safe. With all of this to fathom, and all the terror to feel, I couldn't stop thinking about Steven and Mary and how they would be coping with all this. The good thing was they weren't from here and were probably about to leave the country. Somehow, I knew I had to call him and tell him everything. I got home, packed everything, clothes, laptop, food, everything that might be of use at some point. The plan now was to stay safely with Farah until we found a way out of here. I sat on the edge of the bed to catch my breath and prepare myself to leave. I looked around my room, and somehow the things that were the heart of every problem I was having weren't so bad anymore. I saw the electricity bills I struggled to pay two weeks ago, the work clothes I painfully put on every day, and the resignation letter I half wrote sat on the nightstand. It proved to me that first of all I was a coward because I never had the guts to finish it. Sometimes, we are consumed by the negative things our brain chooses to focus on and we forget that happiness in our lives came from where we chose to look and the way we looked at things around us. I didn't have all the things I dreamed about but at least I felt safe. I felt that I might, at a certain point, change the way my future was being written.

Now everything was slipping away, and every feeling of hope was being replaced with concern and the question "how will this end?".

What will I do now? I probably was a coward and all the decisions I took in my life were proof of that. And what can a coward do? What can someone who was scared of everything do here? I was afraid of change, people, making decisions, chasing goals, and dreams. Everything was scary to me. The fear of failure was all I knew, and it had become a part of who I was.

I was scared, and maybe that word didn't come close to describing how I felt. I was terrified, but this time it needed to be different. I needed to be different. These might be my last days on Earth so I might as well live what I had left as I should have lived what had now gone. I had felt different ever since I met Farah. She made me forget all the failures I was seeing right now, and I realized whenever I was with her I was worth something. The way she looked at me on its own gave me superpowers. And when I was with her I felt invincible and that was how it was going to be. I vowed to myself that, from this moment on, I would be strong for her. I'd be optimistic and wouldn't make her feel alone or sad. Let them bomb the place. Let them terrify everyone. Let them kill everyone. No fear or sadness would make its way into my girl's heart because it had me as its protector. The only way I would be able to survive this was if I had a purpose, and I had chosen mine.

The roads were still empty, and only a few people had the courage to make it out of their homes and inspect what last night had left for us. No stores opened, not even the pharmacies or the bakeries. There was no sign of the police or the military. All I saw was people looking for answers in each other's eyes, and fear and uncertainty were the only answers they got.

"Zayn, mon petit, what are you doing here?"

Ah, a familiar voice with a beautiful face behind it was what I needed right now.

"Madame Jamila, what are you doing outside? I didn't expect to see you here."

"Where did you expect me to be, Zayn, hiding under my bed? I'm here looking around and seeing if my neighbors are okay after last night. How are you? Son, they are successfully taking our city, and the capital gave up on us. I hear that these animals are coming tonight to take full control of the city and…"

"No, Madame, where did you hear that from? It's impossible. The government will probably do something before it lets something like that happen."

"Government, what government, Son? Where are the police? Shouldn't they be here protecting their people? They abandoned all of us and the blood of the people who died is on their hands." The poor old woman finished, with tears in her eyes.

"Wait! People died?"

"Yes, people died. Innocent people, like you and me. People who didn't want to take any part in this vicious fight over land, guns, and power. A family of six left this ugly world we are trapped in when it rained bombs on their house and one of those instruments of war took their lives."

"I don't know what to say. I spoke with my mom early this morning, and she's going to try to come and pick me up."

"Definitely not a good idea, Zayn. It's too dangerous for anyone to try to get in here. They are probably taking control of the roads that lead in and out of the city. They wouldn't allow anyone to leave, and they will probably use us as human shields, just like they did with people in Umailim."

"All of this is sucking the life out of me, I swear, Madame. I don't even know what I'm supposed to do."

"Stay strong. That's the only advice I can give you. It happened too fast for any of us to have prepared for this. I mean, only yesterday I was talking with my friend who wanted to bring her daughter to my house so I can tutor her and help become better at French. We knew something was up, but no one knew that it would escalate this quickly. I'm certain now that it's going to be hard for us, but the only way we can manage to get through this is to believe that it's always darkest before the dawn. I need you to always be hopeful and confident. It's the only thing they can't kill in us and is the only thing that will help us survive."

"I'll try my best, Madame. You stay safe, okay?"

"Take care, Zayn."

Ten

I rang the bell. She opened the door, and with the most beautiful smile ever, she welcomed me in.

"Is everything all right? You look upset."

"I'm okay, Sweetheart. I'm just tired from carrying this heavy suitcase."

"Here, let me help you."

We went in, and together we started to get all the food I brought in the fridge.

"Did you call your parents, Farah? How are they?"

"Oh, Zayn, don't get me started. I was on the phone with them for more than an hour. They are more than worried. I didn't even tell them that Jasmine is sick. They couldn't find a way to get here as the only airport they could land at is the one in the capital, and from what Dad said, it's almost impossible to even get here now because it's partially closed. I told them that I have a friend who is going to come stay with Jasmine and me, and that I might leave with him to go to the capital. Mom was actually relieved when she knew that I'm not alone here. Even my uncle tried to get here yesterday but he went back, barely making it alive when the bombing and explosions started."

"Oh no, I hope he's okay.

"Yes, he's fine. It was just terrifying. Dad said that this is a war zone now. I swear I don't even know what that means."

"There isn't a single soldier outside, or even the police. They all left us in the hands of the mercenaries."

"Exactly. My dad explained it to me a little bit. The government lost yesterday's fight because they weren't ready for it, and were taken by surprise. He said they are regrouping and planning how to get their hands back on the city."

"That means more bombing, Farah. People are going to die not knowing who killed them or why they are being killed."

A moment of silence took us both to the place of fear we were both trying not to think about, so I broke that silence with, "The good thing is that I found Nutella back in my house and I know how much you love it. So, now we can survive anything, can't we?"

Her most serious look was quickly replaced by the cutest laughter ever.

"Oh, my dear soulmate, you know me so well, don't you? Thank you for the most beautiful gift ever, which I'm obviously going to eat alone and I'm not going to give you any. So, stop looking at me with those eyes of yours trying to convince me to share!"

"Are you trying to get fat so the terrorists won't bother kidnapping you because you would be too heavy for them to carry?" I was laughing hard, and she was looking around for something to throw at me.

"You are so proud of that joke, aren't you?"

"No, I was just trying to say that your plan won't work anyway, because even if you put on 700 kilos you will always be the prettiest girl I have ever seen. You would be heavy, but pretty," I said, teasing her.

"You are so silly, stop making fun of me," she said, laughing

And that's how Farah and I were. Our lives might be in the balance, but we managed to laugh the fear away. If I showed the strength and bravery of Superman around her, it was only possible because she was my Sun. Sometimes, I looked at her and became lost for words, and I wouldn't say how adorable, and amazing she was. No! She was all of that, but I got lost for words because I couldn't thank her enough for saying "Hi" to me that day in the library. I couldn't thank her enough for the happiness she brought into my life, and I couldn't be grateful enough for having her as the light that brightened the dark tunnel that was my world. And you know who was just as beautiful as Farah? Jasmine. She was her sister, so obviously, she had her older sibling's charm and beauty, but the little girl was too smart for her age. I could tell she was going to grow up to be an amazing person. I loved spending time with her. I didn't know that the little girl loved reading books, but when she saw me she asked me to sit next to her and explained how she needed to finish her book so she could start writing a resume about it, because her teacher asked them to and she wanted to have the best resume as she always did. I was looking at her and tears were trying to climb their way into my eyes because the little angel didn't actually get what was happening outside. She didn't realize that she probably wouldn't be at school again for goodness knew how long. The innocence I saw in her eyes was probably what this war was going to kill in her first, and it wasn't fair.

The world we live in isn't fair. An eleven-year-old girl

should be asking questions such as when they were going to get their favorite new toy, or could they have ice cream late at night and that was it. The hunger for power that we were the victims of was going to kill that innocence, and it was going to be replaced with screams of fear and howls of, "Please, God, don't take me now."

We spent the rest of the day just having fun and enjoying each other's company. It was quiet outside, which helped us forget the mess we were in. Farah and I cooked together. I made pizza again, and she made us dessert; cupcakes to be exact, and they were amazing if you didn't count the first time when she had to throw all of it away because they sank in the middle.

I tried to convince her that they were good enough to eat, but she wouldn't even allow me to taste them. She kept on saying, "it's not my fault, it's the oven's fault. So, you had better forget this ever happened or I will end you right here." Of course, I didn't forget and teased her about it all night. We watched three movies and all of them were anime as Jasmine was elected the TV queen that night, and controlled what we were going to watch. We stayed up late. Well, Farah and I did, our queen slept before the third movie even finished. Although it was her favorite one, the little princess couldn't fight it anymore and used my chest as her pillow and my arm as her teddy bear. She was the cutest thing I had ever seen trying to find comfort in a very uncomfortable position. She refused to go to her room because, and I quote, "If I leave, you guys are going to have fun without me, and I can't allow that."

I held her close and prayed to God that he would keep her safe and pull us all out of this. On the other hand, my soulmate and I were having all sorts of conversations. I didn't know what time it was, but the stars were high up there watching over us. Looking at her, wondering who this person was who has more charm and glow than all the rest of us combined, we were arguing about who was the better chef, Gordon Ramsay, or Jamie Oliver. We both agreed that the only way we could settle this was by going to London and visiting their restaurants and then deciding who was better. We dreamt about the different days we were hoping to see. We dreamt about the vacations we would take together, and the places we would visit. We imagined the food we would taste, the concerts we would attend. Every thought and speculation led us to agree that as long as we were doing something together it will be worth dying for.

I looked at the clock hanging on the wall as I opened my eyes, and it pointed at 4:24 am. I woke to the sound of helicopters flying over our heads. My heart started to beat fast and I didn't know what to do. It was obvious now that it was the second round of whatever happened the previous night. Was this the military trying to scout the place and look for the houses the terrorists were hiding in? The answer didn't take long to come, and I started to hear the sound of explosions and bombs demolishing the silence we had enjoyed all day. I held jasmine really tight and tried to cover her ears so she wouldn't wake up to the horror scene we were in. I looked at Farah, and she was looking at me horrified by the deathly sound we were hearing. We looked at each other and our eyes were the only gate to the feelings we had inside. She started crying, and I sat there helplessly trying to wipe the tears off her face, trying to hide the truth that we saw very clearly in front of us. Every second could be it now, every breath could be our last, and every missile we heard being fired could have our names on it.

"Farah, come here!" I whispered.

She made her way next to me and I put my arm around her trying to make her feel safe, trying to form an imaginary shield from the dangers that were surrounding us.

"Don't cry, dear, we'll be fine, it's going to be all right, I promise. Do you think that God would allow his angel to get hurt, or for our queen to be scared?"

She smiled through all her tears and said, "Asking me to stop crying while you have tears in your eyes isn't very convincing."

"I'm only tearing up because these explosions outside are making it very hard for you to hear my heart beating loudly and screaming vehemently with happiness because I'm surrounded by the sweetest humans to ever exist."

She got even closer, sat her head right above my heart, and said, "It's okay, I can hear it now, and it's all I need."

The whole night was me holding on to the two people dearest to my heart right then. We didn't sleep, we didn't even talk, we just froze. You can't find any words to say when all you feel is fear and all you sense is the ground vibrating after every blast you hear.

I never was a believer and never prayed that much, even though after my father passed away my mom tried her best to implant that seed of faith in my heart. She thought that the love I would feel for God could actually get me out of the hole that Dad's death had left me in. I remember the days that she spoke to me about the miracles praying could get you. I remembered the hours we spent reading the holy book, learning about God's mercy upon humanity. I also remembered every time we put our hands together to pray. I always had a question not a prayer: why did you take him away from me? However, I think she successfully planted that faith in me because in a moment of despair like this I found myself begging God to show me that mercy she always spoke about and protect and help us live through all of this. I kept wondering what kind of world we were living in. I was pleading and urging God to keep us safe from the people who were trying to take our lives, in His name as well. Who were these people fighting for, and whose hands would the blood of those who died taint?

No God would command his worshipers to commit crimes in his name. No God worth loving would demand that people be killed in his name. The whole idea behind believing in a lord and a maker was the search for a higher purpose and guidance so the believer could rise above the sins and the demons that try to crawl their way into their soul. This was the devil's work we all feared, and this was the fear and blood that makes him rise above us all.

Eleven

Four weeks passed, and the only thing that changed was the fact that we started to get used to everything that was happening around us. We gave up on the idea that we were going to make it out of there back to the normal world. The plague was already everywhere, and no one was there to help. The government's genius plan to get the city back was to bomb every place the rebels might be in. Every house, every building, every corner was a target for their missiles. No one was brave enough to come and see what it was like on the ground, and the armed militias took advantage of the situation. They occupied all the houses that were abandoned by their previous owners after they left and ran for their lives when all of this started. Houses that were once a place of warmth, a place where memories were engraved on the walls with the laughter and love those families shared, were now snake holes with venom being stored and death being prepared for all of us to taste. They implemented their own laws and they came with their own rules that were slowly being uncovered every day we spent in this hellhole. Everyone had to behave a certain way now. Clothes were very important to these animals, and you had to look, talk, operate like one of them if you wanted to live. The message that we all learned from day one was that we didn't mean anything to them. If you didn't obey the rules you were choosing the wrong path and defying God's plan for you. But, reading between the lines, they were trying to use us. We were human shields and a distraction that they could use to deflect their enemies' focus from their horrendous actions.

Doctors, teachers, plumbers, students were all the same now. We all gave up the goals and dreams we had previously, and these were now replaced with a single goal. The first symptom of the disease we were all cursed with was the fact that we lined up in front of the bakery every day to get a piece of bread that we had to survive on until the next day's sun shone on top of our heads, in the same place, doing the same thing. They controlled the bakeries, the pharmacies, and the hospitals. Everything we might need to survive was in their hands, and more than that, they went to every house in the city collecting information on the people who lived there. When they came to Farah's place, I had to pretend that she and Jasmine were my sisters, and I was there to take care of them as an older brother. That day was probably one of the scariest days we had encountered so far. It was horrible, especially when one of the hounds opened his mouth and said, "You better stay close to your family now. You don't know when we might need soldiers and you are a strong man. You could be a terrific addition to our army, where you can finally find your purpose and serve the Lord that blessed you with everything you have."

The sad part was my response, "Whatever you want, sir. "

A part of me wanted to jump at him and gouge his eyes out with my fingers, but I was looking at Farah, and she was giving me that 'don't you dare do anything stupid look' and I wasn't going to anyway. I had seen what they had done to Omar when he said 'no'. Omar used to be a doctor who lived with his mother across the street from Farah, and she had known him for a long time. Being a doctor for so many years, and probably saving so many people made it hard for him to accept what our world had come to, and that we needed a kind of saving now that he wasn't capable of providing. They knew that he was a doctor, and to them he was an asset. One day, after the government hit them really hard, bombarding one of their underground compounds and hitting a large number of their armed puppets, they were looking for all the help they could get. So, they went to him and asked him to join them and provide medical assistance for their wounded troops. The bravery I saw in his eyes was something that I will always remember. Twelve of them were standing in front of him and he just said 'no'. I think he was the first one to ever say no to them since they arrived. He was so composed and spoke the truth, "I swore an oath the day I graduated, and it was to help all the people who were in need of any form of medical assistance. YOU!" And he pointed at every one of them. "You don't deserve to live because you aren't even human, so go crawl back to the hell you came from and burn. I hope you all burn!"

We were watching from the window, and I was holding Farah's hand, hoping the worst wouldn't happen, but expecting them to beat him up, shoot, torture, or even kill him, but they didn't. Two of them held him down, tied his hands behind his back, and another monster went inside his house. They grabbed his mother and dragged her out of her wheelchair until she was right in front of him. He was screaming, and they were laughing. He was begging, and they were amused to see the fear in his eyes. He screamed, and we watched them break him down with words rather than action, "You think you are so special now, don't you? Do you think we won't find doctors who will help us? With all the years you studied, you should have learned to bow down and accept that power always wins over the stupid bravery you are trying to hold on to," one of them said.

His mother was looking at him screaming, breaking down in front of them as she tried to calm him down, "Son, it's going to be all right," she said, trying to get closer to him.

She was on all fours and they were pushing her around with their feet, but that brave mother wouldn't let go of her son's face as she screamed louder than their laughter, "Don't you bow down to them, Son. I didn't raise you to be a coward! Your father is looking over us now, and the worst thing that they think could happen to us is the best thing we were hoping for all these years. We will get to see him and live as happily as we once were before he left. Smile, Son, smile, baby…"

The screaming stopped, and a terrifying silence took over the place until it was broken by the birds flying and shrieking from the horror they had witnessed. Drops of rain started to fall, proving to us that even the sky cries after watching hatred win. The raindrops mixed with his mom's tears in a desperate attempt from the clouds to wipe the sadness from the woman's heart. She smiled in silence… and he cried in pain.

They shot his mom twenty centimeters away from him and her blood covered his face. They took her life, and we all saw his soul leave his body as he spoke, "Mom, I'm sorry, please forgive me. Mom, I love you! Please don't go anywhere, don't leave me, please, Mom. What will I do without you?"

And those were the last words that came out of his mouth, as he crumbled in her arms, trying to hug what was left of her, and when they untied him one of the bastards looked at Omar laying in his mom's blood and said, "I think she might need your medical assistance now, or is it too late, Doctor?"

They took off, leaving him there in the middle of the street sobbing, not being able to move, crippled by what they took from him. Like the grim reaper, they collected his will to live but left his body to feel the pain of its absence.

Just like that, we all knew who we were dealing with, and it became clear that defiance wasn't an option. I hugged Farah. I hugged what I still had left in this world, and in a moment of complete anger, I spoke, "I hope I die a million deaths, and my body is sacrificed to the devil they worship before I see you suffer like that."

You can grieve, you can cry, you can feel sad, but you must move on and keep going with the hope that one day you will be free. Free to either continue your days on this earth trying to forget and move on or free to stand before God and ask him why he put you through that. My mother was one of the ropes that kept my soul from falling even deeper in the ocean of despair. Now we didn't have electricity, no TV, no fridge, no heat, nothing, and there wasn't even a place you could get food from anymore. They controlled all resources that were left in the city, the supermarkets, the stores, the butchers, bakers, and even the fruiterers were in their hands and weren't allowed to sell anything without their approval. We were now prisoners in our homes, prisoners suffering the torture of not being dead yet. If you don't crack under fear you will under hunger and starvation. So, every day I went to the only bakery they allowed us to go to and I had to walk for more than ten kilometres just for a loaf of bread. We had to stand in lines like hungry dogs waiting for our turn to get the food we came for and leave without even saying a word to anyone or even look at each other.

All of this even shook Uncle Jamal's confidence and he started to feel as lost as we all did. Today I had said to myself that I needed to go and say hi to him and see how he was doing. It had been more than ten days since I saw him, and I missed the wise defiant words that he always said to me. In circumstances like these, you need to be reminded to stay strong, to be who you are and to never forget that you are the one who is in control of your fate, and you are the one who decides it.

"Farah, I'm going to see Uncle Jamal, then I'll go get the pizza and I'll be back."

We called that stupid piece of bread they gave us pizza and laughed every day when I came home, and she said, "Did you get me my favorite, Zayn?"

And of course, I answered, "Honey, how can I forget. Pepperoni and extra cheese, mixed with tears of sadness coming from a terrorist's eye because of what they feel inside."

It was sad, I know, but it made us laugh and laughter was one of the ways that made us feel safe around each other. Everything could change, but at least we will always have that."

"Okay, Zayn, take care. Don't be late."

I was putting on my coat when Farah yelled, "I knew that you would forget. How dare you?"

I laughed and tried to dodge the question.

"I was testing you, and the good thing is that you successfully passed the test, so come here."

"You are such a fish, Mister." she said, as she got close to me.

We had a deal that whenever I left the house we had to pinkie promise that I come back to her safe and sound. I also needed to give her three kisses on her forehead. One was for the past that we needed to let go of, one for the present that we hated and hopefully together we would manage to get away from, and one for the future that we were dreaming to have together. It was something that we held on to and what was funny about it was that every time we did it, Jasmine would scream, "Me too, me too, me too." It was our little thing, a desperate, family treat that we all lived on and that we couldn't give up, especially the little princess who brightened our lives more than the sun above us.

The city didn't look like it used to anymore. Most of the buildings and skyscrapers had been destroyed in the first couple of days of this bomb fest. Even the place where I used to work was barely standing now. I walked past it every day on my way to the bakery and good God, I never thought I'd say this, but I missed my copying machine and the desk that I thought was sucking the life out of me. I had hated it but now I missed it and wished I could go back to sitting behind it, invisible to the people around me. I wondered how they all were sometimes. I had lost contact with almost all of them after what happened, except Steven and even with him it had been more than a month since we spoke. I knew that he was still here but in the other side of the city. We didn't get a chance to talk much, but I knew that Mary made it out of the country and that he was trying to leave as well.

Steven was half-Italian, and his government was trying to get him out of here. The only problem was that the airport had been destroyed and no planes could land anywhere near, but almost all the embassies and consulates were secretly trying to get their people out. That's what he told me, he just had to lay low, and his presence shouldn't be noticed. They would consider capturing people like him the greatest catch possible. They could use him either to send a message by having his head cut off live on YouTube, for all the world to see, sending fear and disgust to all the souls who were bravely feeling our pain through their actions, or they could pressure his government to pay for his freedom, and either way they win.

Uncle Jamal, on the other hand, was still trying to keep the image of the strong, powerful individual whom we could all go to, to feed off his energy. But a couple of days ago, he showed bravery like none of us had seen before. The devils came to him with a deal that involved him giving up and leaving his café in exchange for security protection and lots of money. The café was in the center of the city in a very crowded neighborhood, exactly on the intersection of the two main roads that lead in and out of the purgatory we are in. The streets in front were always packed with civilians and if you got on the roof of the building you would be able to cover almost every road in the city. Their deal was simple. They wanted to turn it into some sort of a chamber of command, one that wouldn't be discovered quickly, and they would use the people's presence and the huddled avenues as a cover from the drones the government kept on sending to spy on them.

He said, "No."

He screamed, "Hell, no!"

He was one of the few brave men who had the guts to say 'no' to them and live afterwards. He kicked them out! If I didn't see it myself I wouldn't have believed it. He threw them out of his place pushing every single one of them, not caring about the guns they kept pointing at his head.

"I would rather burn it to the ground with me inside before I let any of you animals step foot inside this place." He howled like a wolf defending his territory and none of us knew why they let him live after that. They just retreated and upon going, one of them pulled out a C4 charge and said, "We will see about that, old man."

"Just bring it and we will see who gets burnt, you bastard."

The old man was a hero in a cape after that day, for all of us, and his presence was a blessing for the weak among us.

"Uncle Jamal, are you here?" I said, walking into the café.

"Zayn, don't come in here it's all dusty. I'm cleaning the back room. I'll be right there."

I noticed a different tone in his voice. I didn't know what it was, but I felt as if he was hiding something, or just afraid of me seeing him in whatever shape he was in. It wasn't long before he showed up covered in dust, wearing his crooked glasses, and holding a small, wooden box that he put on the counter as he pulled out a chair and sat next to me.

"Uncle, are you okay, what's wrong?

He had a towel on his shoulder that he used to wipe the sweat off his forehead as he took off his glasses and looked at me with a gaze that I'd never seen him wear before.

"Uncle, what's wrong, is the family okay?"

"They got to me, Zayn, these godless creatures knew how to break me! I have packed everything and I'm leaving my little world with all that it was. They kidnapped my son's little daughter, Sarah. She's only eight-years-old! They took her from her mother's hand in the middle of the busy street as they were on their way to the bakery. Everyone watched, but no one was able to do anything as they put her in the trunk of their car and drove off, leaving her mother on the ground in a puddle of tears. Yesterday, they came here offering her safe return in exchange for this place, and I said 'yes', Son. I said 'yes' to giving up all I have left in this world.

"You see these four walls, Son? They were witness to all the events that shaped me into the man I am today. These four walls saw me get ready to go ask my wife's father for her hand. That counter saw me hide behind it and cry with happiness when my son was born.

"Every penny I had was invested to keep this place going over the years. Even now, after everything that has happened, I still wake up early in the morning and I still open the place knowing that there will be no customers. But mopping these floors gave me a reason to smile and made me feel that I still exist. And now, I'm going to give it all away, so they can use it to kill our people, to kill me, you, and everyone we care about. I wish I had died before I felt this pain. What am I supposed to do now, go home and sit around waiting for the sweet release of death?" He looked down and used the piece of cloth to wipe the tears that he wasn't able to hold in anymore.

"All my life, I took care of this place, and it did the same for me. It gave my purpose, it nourished my soul, and it felt like one of the very few places where I was safe.

"I'm willing to die for the little angel they took away from us. I never even loved her father as much as I love her, but she is going to come back to a world where everything can be compromised out of fear. They can have everything they want from us because they know that we are afraid of them. All of us have something that we consider too precious to lose and that's where we become the victims."

"Uncle, unfortunately there is nothing I can say that can make you feel better, but they didn't break you, they can't break you. You are this town's hero, Uncle. All of us here turn to you for advice, for help, and guidance. And yes, this place gave you purpose, but you have one outside as well. I can't count the times I was on the verge of breaking and you talking to me and guiding me through the unpaved road that my life was taking me down is something that I'll never forget. Let me tell you something, Uncle. I lived all my life without a father, without that person you can run to looking for answers, and you were that person for me, just as you are for many other people here. Leave here, but know that you will one day come back free, free from this fear they are controlling us with, free like we once were."

"We were never free, Son, we were just pretending to be. I'm not young anymore. I don't even know if I'm going to make it back here. But if I don't, promise me that after we pull through this, no matter how long it takes us, you will come back here and you will remember and keep reminding people here what this place was and what its owner wanted it to be. I couldn't ask that from my own son because I know after what happened to his daughter he is going to leave and he wouldn't have the heart to come back and see what his father gave up for him."

"I promise you, Uncle. I promise that we will walk in here together, and if we don't, this place and these people will know that joy was felt in here. That love was spread from here and that sacrifices were made to free our loved ones from this fear."

"Thank you, Son, you should go to the bakery before it's too late."

"I'm going, but promise me, Uncle, that you will be okay."

"I will never be okay after this, but I'll pretend that I am. I can only promise you that."

My heart broke into a million pieces looking at what this man was going through. Every one of us was going through a struggle that was forced upon him. My mother, who I would probably never see again, Farah and her parents, Omar and his mother, Uncle Jamal and me. I wondered who would make it out of here alive, who would be lucky enough to survive and who would physically and emotionally be able to continue when everything around them died.

"Zayn, wait!" I turned around to see Uncle Jamal stand and walk towards me.

"Son, I have a way of getting you out of here. I'm certain now that this life here isn't for you. You need to leave and start afresh, even if you have to start from way down at the bottom. I have a friend who is a fisherman and has been sneaking people out of this hellhole. He uses his boat and the cover of night to ride the waves to Cyprus, and from there you can choose to go either to Italy or to Turkey. It's a long, dangerous trip, Son, but it can lead to a new beginning out of here."

"Uncle, I don't know what to say, apart from thank you so much. I have been trying to find a way out, so I'll take it with all the danger that comes with it. I don't care, but the thing is that it's not just me here, Uncle. I have two people who, if I leave, need to go with me. I can't leave them here."

"Son, this isn't a trip where you can take your friends with you! If I can manage to fit you, and only you in, it would be a miracle on its own. I have been trying to get my son and his family out for more than a month, and only last week he confirmed that he has a spot for them. Keep in mind that I paid a ton of money for it. They are leaving next week, but for you we have to wait and see where there will be another opening and another opportunity like this. So, if I say you are going alone, you are!"

He had become really annoyed when I mentioned not being able to go alone and started to speak to me in a very serious, loud tone.

"Uncle, you know that I love you like a father, but if you ask me to leave without Farah and her sister you might as well kill me right now and feed my body to the stray dogs outside. I won't go without them, no matter what happens. And if it's written in the stars for me to die here I'll gladly accept it with open arms as long as I have the possibility of seeing Farah before I go."

"Who is this Farah that you are throwing away the chance of a bright future for? You never said anything about her."

"I can't describe what she means to me, Uncle, but imagine the best thing that ever happened to you and multiply it by infinity. We met by pure luck, Uncle, and I have been living in her house since the bombing started. Her parents got trapped in Italy and they couldn't come back here, and we have been keeping each other safe and I..."

"Is she worth throwing this chance away, Zayn. This might never happen again, and then you will be here forever. You might die here for heaven's sake. There will always be Farahs for you to meet." He screamed at me, and I couldn't resist yelling back.

"There won't! And don't you dare even think that I will leave her here! I don't care about leaving or living. When I was dead inside, she was the one who brought me back to life, and you can take me on a boat to the heavens in the seventh sky and it wouldn't compare to what she is to me." I realized that I was shouting at the old man, so I tried to compose myself as he annoyed me even more with his question.

"Is this a joke to you?"

"Uncle, please understand, I'm sorry for yelling, but please understand. Let me ask you how you feel about your son's daughter? The one you are giving all of this away for."

"What do you mean, how do I feel? I love her more than anything."

"Exactly. If I said I loved Farah more than anything it still wouldn't be close enough to describing how I feel about her. You are a firm believer in God right, Uncle? Now imagine if you prayed for something all your life and one day you woke up and it was right there in front of you, but not like you imagined it would be. No, it was a billion times better. Now, Farah isn't the thing you prayed for. She is that overwhelming feeling of gratefulness you would feel towards God for giving you what you want. She is the closest thing to happiness that I ever felt. She is like the light that goes through these windows lighting up the place, like the oxygen we live on, and like the heavens we are promised. You know me, Uncle, you know how lonely I was. And I'm sorry, but I lied about my job. It wasn't that fancy, and I never was important at that company. I was the closest thing to the clock on the wall there. They only looked at me when they needed documents to be copied and unimportant things to be done. I was invisible for as long as I can remember, and then I met her and started seeing colors I never knew existed.

"She isn't my girlfriend or my lover, no, she's way above that. You see, Uncle, you can break up with your partner, and you can divorce your wife, but I can never even picture a life where she isn't the diamond my world revolves around. I don't want to say I love her! That word is scary to me because people are used to falling out of love just as they fall into it. I will never be able to explain how I feel about her, and I'm not expecting you to understand. I thank God every day for making us go through this hell, because if it wasn't for this I would have never got the chance to be happy. Believe it or not, I'm happy. I'm scared, no I'm terrified, but I'm happy and I could die and stand before God tomorrow with a smile on my face that she drew, and I'll beg him to make me go through this hell again just so I feel what it's like to be touched by her soul and for my heart to beat just from seeing her smiling. So don't ever think that I would leave her for a safer place that wouldn't exist without her. NEVER!"

I stopped talking only to see him looking at my boiling-red face with the biggest smile on his face. I think he understood exactly what I meant, and the mix of tears and loud noises I made were the perfect guide for that.

"Son, it's okay. You should be proud; not many people get to feel what you are feeling now. Some of us spend a lifetime looking for a person worthy of the description you gave of this girl, so you should be really blessed for having her. Through the story your tears wrote talking about her I can happily say that maybe you found your purpose, so go ahead and keep it safe until we figure a way out."

I tried to apologize one more time and left embarrassed

after putting on a show for the brave, old man. I got to the bakery, and it felt as if I arrived there late. There were at least three hundred people, and it was horrible. When I was young, I used to watch those documentaries about very poor countries in Africa suffering from famine and diseases, and I always wondered how it felt to be there, and how those people felt. I never thought in a million years that a day would come when I would be living that life. That was the only thing I kept thinking about as I was watching people fight, push, and scream at each other, and for what? For a piece of bread that isn't that edible anyway. It was a horrible scene that I had to stare at from afar until I had enough courage to jump in the middle of the battleground. I had to get in there and fight my way in, stepping on the weak, and ignoring the elderly, just so I could manage to get us something to eat.

I left the wrestling arena with at least three bruises on my face and a couple of scratches on my hands from people trying to snatch the bread out of my grip. I was very lucky, because after I left the bakery closed its doors, leaving hundreds of angry, hungry people. There was never enough bread for everyone, and I thought the people who controlled the bakery had specific orders to keep some of us hungry. It was easier to control people with empty stomachs. They will do anything to kick that hunger away or to see their loved ones fed. The good thing is that I made it out alive and kind of happy because I could go back to Farah with pizza just as I promised. That feeling actually had me start a conversation with myself, *Zayn, what are you feeling right now? Did you just hit a new low? You are happy because you bought a loaf of bread.*

I laughed, knowing there was no answer for that, but it made me think about what happiness really is. Wasn't it that feeling of joy we all keep looking for from the moment we are born? When we were young it was very easy for us to feel that, but as we grew up and opened our eyes to the world around us things changed, and it just became something we chased. For some people, happiness is a job or a position, for others it's money, maybe a car or a villa. It might be success or personal achievement for many, but now and after going through this I thought I had a clear answer, it wasn't as ea…

"Pretty boy, stop right there."

I didn't know where the voice was coming from, and honestly, I didn't want to, so I tried to keep my head down and continue on my way home.

"I said stop right there or you'll regret it."

I turned around only to see three guys looking at me with an evil stare that made my whole body shiver. I had a feeling that this was going to take a turn for the worst, so I turned around and as I was about to start running out of there three more guys popped from around the corner and stood in front of me.

"It's rude to ignore someone talking to you, my friend." One of them said that as he kept waving the steel pipe he had in his hand.

"I'm sorry, I didn't think you were talking to me, sir."

"Oh, I was talking to you, my friend. Tell me, how are you? Is everything all right?"

"I'm okay, sir, just trying to survive like we all are."

"Indeed, we are. Speaking of survival, I see you have something I might need." And he pointed at the piece of bread that was in my hand

"I'm sorry, sir, but I can't give you this. I have a family depending on me and they need this. I'm sorry."

"He has a family that depends on him! I'm so touched by this, I swear I think I'm going to cry. As a matter of fact, I want to give you my piece of bread. Whoops, I don't have any. Isn't that a shame. But that means my family will starve. Now tell me, is a good boy like you going to allow that?"

"I'm sorry, please don't do this."

"Now look, there are two choices for you to choose from. Either you give me that bread and you call it a bad day and keep on walking home to your beloved family, or are you going to be stubborn like you are right now, which might piss my friends off, and then I won't be able to stop them. So, you choose, pretty boy, what do you want?"

"Please, sir, don't do this. I'll buy you bread tomorrow, I swear, just please let me take it to my family."

My heart was beating out of my chest, and I was terrified at what was about to happen, but I would never willingly give it to them.

"I'm counting to three. One, two..."

Before he finished, I tried to make a run for it, and before my feet started to move I felt a blow to the back of my head that dropped me to the ground and they started to hit me with everything they had as he screamed, "You see what happens when you don't listen. I didn't want it to be like this, but you have to learn that survival is for the fittest, my friend."

I opened my eyes to an old woman's silhouette trying to talk to me. I couldn't hear anything and could barely see; everything was so bright. I tried to get up, but I couldn't. I looked around me and the only thing I recognized was the blood that covered everything around me.

The woman helped me make it to my feet, "It's okay, Son. They beat you up for the bread you were carrying. That's the world we live in now."

I couldn't help myself, but I started crying. Not because of the pain I was feeling, but for the fact that for the first time in my life I felt that I was weak, as if I were a worthless piece of nothing. As the tears fell on my face, it started to hurt even more. I stood there not knowing what to do or where to go.

"Don't cry, Son, you couldn't have done anything better. They were determined to take it from you no matter what. I'm sorry, I was watching from around the corner and couldn't help you. I was afraid they would take mine as well, but here, let's split this in half."

"No, Ma'am, please I can't take it."

"I insist. I wasn't going to eat all of it anyway. I'm an old lady as you can see and I live alone. I lost my son two weeks ago when the first air strikes took place. He died in my arms, and when I saw you, you reminded me of him and of how brave he was. Please, take this half."

I could barely talk from how much my face was swollen. I couldn't even say thank you. She kept tapping me on my shoulder trying to help make me feel better, saying that everything would be all right.

"Can you make it home by yourself?"

"Yes I can. I'll never forget this, Ma'am."

I took the half she offered and limped back home. Every bone in my body felt broken and I could barely breathe. Blood covered my face, and tears were making it hard for me to see. It was already three hours past the time I was supposed to get back, and Farah was probably more than worried right now. God, what was this life we were living now? I felt certain we needed to get away from here as fast as we could.

My mother tried everything to help us get out of here

but she failed. Farah's uncle tried to come pick us up himself numerous times but stopped after she begged him not to try any more as his life was in greater danger every time he did. What was I supposed to do? God, please get me out of here. Are you even there anymore? Do you still see us or did you give up just like everyone else did? I didn't sign up for any of this, I just wanted to live a normal, boring life. I don't think that I did anything bad to deserve this punishment, so please, God, you either take me out of here or take my life. Please, I can't stand this anymore. For now, I can still accept everything you are throwing at me, but I don't think I can if it happened to Jasmine or Farah, so please answer me. Damn it, answer!

I fell to the ground. I was giving up. I couldn't take this anymore. Screams of pain and fear filled the empty road I was in. I was just tired. Lord help me out of here.

I stayed like that until I felt it getting darker and had to get up. Darkness, as we knew, brought death from above, so I got up and kept walking.

I was a couple of meters away from the door when I heard it opening and Farah running towards me. She started to scream at me. I think she was upset with how late I was, so I kept my head down so she couldn't see my face until she was standing in front of me.

"Zayn, look at me!"

"I'm sorry, Farah I really di…"

"I said look at me, goddamn it."

I did, and as much as seeing her face eased my pain and suffering, her seeing mine did the absolute opposite. She kept staring at me with a look of disbelief, and I had to interrupt, "Let's get in, Farah, it's not safe here."

She helped me get inside the house, and as soon as she closed the door I fell to the ground, screaming with agony and crying from this painful suffering our life had turned into. She was trying to help me get up and the only thing I could remember was her tears falling on my face as she held my head between her arms.

"Zayn, I'm sorry, please forgive me. I don't know what to do, please get up, please, Zayn, answer me. You are okay, right? You pinkie promised me that we were going to get through this together, so you need to be okay, you need to keep your promise. I swear, without you I'll fall apart. In this hell we are trapped in you are my heaven, so please get up. God! Help me please! I need him to be safe, you can't take him away from me!"

I didn't know where I was or what time it was when I opened my eyes only to see Farah sleeping on a chair on the right side of the bed I was in. I tried to move without waking her up but as soon as I lifted my arm pain blew my cover with a scream that I tried to hide. Farah opened her eyes and from how red they were I knew that she probably spent all night crying. She helped me sit in the bed and brought me pills and water.

"I'm sorry for putting you through this."

"Shut up please, Zayn. Save your energy. Here, you have to take these. I went to Omar last night and he was kind enough to come and help me get you in bed. He checked your whole body for broken bones, but fortunately he didn't find any, just lots and lots of bruises everywhere. He had some pain sedatives that his mother used to take, together with some antibiotics. Thank God he was here. I freaked out when I saw you like that, Zayn. You have no idea. There isn't a hospital that I can take you to and the bombing and air strikes started almost an hour after you got back. I just want to know what happened, Zayn, Who did this to you?

"It was over the loaf of bread I bought for us. Some guys tried to take it from me, and when I didn't give it up this happened. I passed out for more than three hours on the side of the road until one amazing old lady stopped and woke me up."

"What? I can't believe this. Are we there now, all of this for a piece of bread?"

"Farah, I don't care about this. All I care about now is that we need to get out of this city and maybe even this country. I don't know how but we need to."

"As long as I'm with you I don't care. I'd go to the deepest part of hell if you asked me to. After all, I'm the reason this happened to you today. The bread you were getting was mainly for my sister and me, you barely even touch it."

"Oh, please stop. You, me, jasmine, we are one, one family, and no matter how bad things get for us we will manage to pull through. Tomorrow, I'll go to the bakery and buy the bread again. If they stop me I will get beaten up for it again, but that won't stop us from trying to survive. We should never give up. We need to have lunch together like every happy family on the face of this earth does. So don't you say that you caused any of this. The only reason I made it here with all the pain I was feeling was you. I needed to get back to my source of oxygen and to see the light again. No matter how broken my body felt, I knew that seeing your face alone could heal me. I'll have you remember I'm invincible."

"Okay, you need to go back to sleep and have some rest because I think you're starting to describe someone else. I'll be here if you need anything."

"Stop being silly, I'm serious." I said, laughing as I finished, "What time is it anyway?"

"It's 4:45 am, the sun is about to rise. I think that's why the bombing stopped."

"You can't sleep in that chair like that! How long have you been sitting there anyway?"

"Ever since yesterday, but I'm okay, stop worrying about me please."

"Farah, come, there's plenty of space in the bed. After all, it's yours, so you're the one who should be sleeping in it."

"No! You need to be comfortable. Omar insisted that you shouldn't move."

"Farah, do you see that window there?"

"Yes, what's wrong with it?"

"I'll jump out of it if you don't come here right now!"

She laughed for the first time that night, and I moved a little bit to the left and said, "You can use my arm as a pillow, come here."

I'm a very stubborn person and she knew that more than anyone else did. She knew this was a fight she could never win, so Her Highness slowly made it into the bed, trying as hard as she could not to cause me any pain. She was looking at me from very close with her beautiful healing eyes, and saw right through me when I tried to hide the fact that my arm was hurting me when she laid her head on top of it.

"How are you feeling, Mister-Use-My-Arm-For-Comfort?"

"I'm okay, what do you mean! That face I just made was just to scare you!"

"Oh, stop it! Can you move, please? Just a little bit."

She gently slid her arm underneath my head and pulled

me closer to her, holding me in a position I had never felt more comfortable in. I felt her heartbeat. I heard the sound that had kept me alive so far and I had never felt safer in my life. I felt at home. It was the first time we were this close, and not only had my soul found its mate, apparently my body had found its Elysium.

With every gasp of air she took, God breathed life in me, and her hair that gently tickled my nose every time she moved helped me forget my pain and suffering. I guessed I was truly invincible.

Twelve

Three scars on my forehead were what I was left with from that horrible day. I spent more than ten days in bed crying myself to sleep every night from the pain I was feeling. If it wasn't for Omar, who came almost every day and regularly checked on my body, I would have probably given up for sure.

I couldn't talk about becoming healthy again without talking about the reason I held on for. The one and only drug that found its way through every fiber of my body and made it its home. Farah! My greatest addiction and my only cure. She was more than a soulmate, more than a best friend, and more than a guardian angel or a caretaker. If I was feeling okay, she would sit next to me and we would talk and laugh, and she would play word games with Jasmine with me as the referee. It was more than a relief to me and more than annoying to her because I always took my little queen's side, and Farah always lost. We laughed as if there was no tomorrow, and the only thing that would stop us from having fun was me screaming from the pain I was under when my body wanted to put me through hell at times. Pain came unwelcomed at the most random times ever, and the only good thing that came with it was seeing my remedy try her best to make me feel better. There was no real medication that I took, so she would sit next to me, hold my hand, and silently cry until I either stopped screaming or just fell asleep. And only then would she roll into a bubble and sleep next to me so when I woke up she would be there if I needed anything.

As soon as I was able to leave the house, I went to see Uncle Jamal. I was hoping that he would be okay, was curious, and scared to see his place and what had happened to it. The answer came not long after I took the turn that led to his café. The whole neighborhood had changed. He wasn't there anymore, and the place was infested with the parasites that were rapidly growing and taking over our city.

I went past the bakery that used to provide the bread we lived on and was choked from seeing our source of food turned into a pile of dust and rubble. I asked around, trying to find out who did it, only to get the sad answer that the government destroyed every facility that might be of use to the people here. They decided that since they couldn't get the rebels out, they were going to kill them all in here, not caring about the children, women, men who were trapped unwillingly in this cursed war zone. We were war casualties, as they were probably saying on the news. It looked as if everyone had given up on trying to get out of here.

I needed more answers and someone to talk to, so I went to Uncle Jamal's house and prayed on the way that he would still be there. I was walking in a ghost town and barren roads led me to an open door. I walked in after a knock that no one answered, and found him sitting with a group of his friends, and their kids were playing in the garden next to them. I stood there for a minute, enjoying the feeling of happiness that overwhelmed me seeing them in their own world, defying the reality that surrounded us with laughter that was so loud at times it probably confused the grim reaper that stood over the city waiting to take all our lives. What did I miss in the few days I was imprisoned? Did something happen that changed how people looked at this whole mess?

Uncle Jamal didn't take long to notice me standing there, and I thought I would receive more of a warm welcome, but he just looked at me and pointed at an empty chair that was next to him.

I sat and it didn't take long for me to start laughing with them and with that the reason behind all of this happiness became very clear to me. These people had accepted their fate. Most of the jokes were about who was going to die first and how soon would it take for all of us to perish. They were talking about the help that we were promised on the news that never showed up, and about the truce that we were promised but never took place. It was funny because, no matter how harsh it sounded to outsiders, we all saw the funny side of it and we all accepted whatever end the story of our life was going to take.

This is the city of the living dead, I said to myself. People accepted everything and nothing really mattered anymore. There were no rich and poor anymore, and with that the importance of appearance didn't matter either. The only sad thing about it that you could see in some of their eyes was a look of disappointment, a look of defeat and failure that they still had to exist in this world. They still had to wake up to this every morning, and you could accept your fate, but you couldn't hate your present, but deep down we all did.

These people were stripped, not only from their freedom, from food, water, electricity, and their loved ones, but they were stripped from their purpose, from their will and their ambition. And that left everyone with one question, what was worth living for anymore? The answer to that gave all our souls a slow, painful death, because we knew that we meant nothing. And the fact that when you woke up in the morning and were still somehow alive, the first thought that crossed your mind was *let me go out and see who died last night.* See if you lost a friend, a neighbor, a lover, a husband, or maybe the son you love. And it just kept on going. We were all lucky for lasting this long and we were cursed for the same reason.

I got to speak to Uncle Jamal later and it made me feel a lot better to see him happy for the fact that his son safely made it to Italy. It wasn't easy, because they had to go through very rough conditions to get there, but he made it and him and his family were settled in a refugee camp. The circumstances that they were in were far from being great, but he was very happy that they were alive and at least no one was trying to kill them.

I was listening to him trying to put hope and faith back in my heart as he said that he hadn't forgotten about me and that he was still trying to figure a way out of here. He took me inside his house, and we talked for hours. I told him about what happened the other day on the way back home from the bakery, and he tried to cheer me up as much as he could. He disappeared for a while in the other room and came back and surprised me with a box full of what looked like canned food.

"I have been keeping this on the side for you, Zayn. I hope it keeps you going for a while," he said, as I tried to decline, saying that he probably needed it as much as I did, but there was no changing his mind. The old man insisted and said that I needed to be strong and ready for when the time would come for me to move.

The way food got in the city now was only through the relief campaigns that the United Nations organized from time to time, and I was sick and missed the first three that took place. Uncle Jamal didn't see me anywhere, and following the good heart that he had, he knew that I needed it to survive, even though I wasn't there.

I didn't know how he managed to get it because it was dangerous to even get close to the food trucks. Farah tried to go by herself but, after seeing the bruises that Omar came back with, I begged her not to, and I only managed to convince her when I played the 'if you go you won't find me when you come back' card and it worked.

"You have to go now. Please be careful and don't let anyone see you carrying that."

I took the box and ran as fast as I could back home. He was right and I knew that if someone saw me holding this treasure I would probably be shot for it, but what helped was the fact that almost all the streets were empty, and I took advantage of it.

I was almost home when I passed in front of a place that was and will always be very close to my heart, the library that I met my other half in, or at least what is left of it now. The whole neighborhood was absolutely demolished, and the library was no exception.

"What if I go in and see if there are any books left that Jasmine and Farah might enjoy?" I said to myself, knowing that this could go very badly, not from being seen by someone, but because the place could fall apart at any second. Apparently, a bomb fell on the side of the building so only half of it was left and barely standing. I started walking to avoid any trouble but deep down I kept picturing the smile that would be drawn on Farah's face, and believe me it was something worth dying for.

It was impossible to get in through the door because it was sealed with a mountain of dirt and stones. I kept scouting around the place and noticed a hole in the side of the wall, which could actually be my way in. I went ahead and put the box of supplies next to the front door, covered it with leaves and dirt, and started climbing.

My shoulder still hurt but I managed to get inside only to see that the place had already been raided. Everything was upside down. Books were everywhere and it was so dusty. I stumbled my way to the stairs and made it to the first floor, just where all the magic took place. Books were on the floor to the point where they formed some sort of a rug. I walked on and went to Farah's favorite section, which was obviously romantic novels, and started to look around for the best titles she would enjoy.

There were titles from Shakespeare to Paulo Coelho and from Virginia Woolf all the way to Danielle Steel. I was smiling so much because, *Zayn, you found the jackpot!* It was really such a pleasurable feeling of excitement imagining the look on her face when she saw them. Jasmine would definitely love the 'Alex Rider' book collection, as she already had one of them.

I came down the stairs carrying over eighteen books, trying to balance them and not fall flat on my face. I threw them gently one by one, and before I climbed out of there I gave the place one last look, "I will never forget you, Gabi. Once again you made me happy, once again you were there for me," I said to the empty chair she used to sit in.

"I promise you, Gabi, one day, just like the magic these words taught me, and the dreams I dreamt in here with my eyes wide open, I'll be back telling you the best story you ever heard, about how I found my soul inside the beautiful escape you gave us throughout the years.

I jumped out of the library and ran back home, anxious to see the smiles that the two angels would have when they saw what I had brought with me.

"Farah, where are you?" I shouted, as I walked through the door.

"I'm in the living room tidying it up, come in or do you need an invitation, stranger?"

"Our life is a scene from the movie *Apocalypse Now* and you're worried that the house is getting dirty?"

"Instead of your smarty-pants remarks and references, I strongly recommend that you come and help me here."

"Okay, I'm coming, but close your eyes please, I have a surprise for you."

I could hear her laugh as she said, "Well, I wonder what surprise it's going to be. Come in, I've closed my eyes."

I walked into the living room, and she was there sitting on the couch looking as charming as I had ever seen her, with the sun taking advantage of the moment and letting its rays find their way onto her beautiful face.

I put the box on the table and said, "Open your eyes, dear!"

She slowly opened her eyes, looked at the box, and said, "What is this, Zayn? Where did you get it?

"Just stop asking questions and look inside please."

The look on her face as she went through the box was priceless. She was surprised, happy, and overwhelmed at the same time, and a mix of these emotions surfaced on her angelic face. Her cheeks turned red and her eyes started to well up. The thing that I probably admired the most about

Farah was the fact that when you did something she loved or said something that made her feel happy she forgot how to express her feelings. She would stutter and keep on saying thank you until you were angry and told her to stop. Even then she wouldn't. People like her with a pure heart were very rare to find or to understand, so I just looked and admired her.

"Zayn, where did you find all of this and please tell me how can I ever live without you?"

"You can't live without me, dear! Uncle Jamal gave me the box of canned food. He got it for us from one of those relief campaigns that I didn't let you go to. As for the books, I got them from the library. Our library. I went there, and it was almost totally destroyed, Farah. It was very sad to see it like that, but I climbed inside and got these books for you and Jasmine. I know that you read everything we have here, even the cookery books and I feel that you memorized all of them. So, here you go, a new addition to your beloved collection and a couple of books for our little queen so she can enjoy this solitude if that's even possible."

"I don't know what to say, I swear. Thank you, Zayn, thank y…"

"Farah, didn't we talk about these thank yous you keep throwing at me constantly!"

"Oh, God, you are wonderful. We are going to read this together, no doubt starting tonight. I'm going to show this to Jasmine, I bet she is going to go crazy for this. She's talking to our parents upstairs."

"Oh really, the phones are working. I should talk to my mom."

"Yes, but meet me in the kitchen after you finish so we can

cook dinner together. And please say hi to your mom for me, and thank her for bringing you into this world."

I went outside to the garden and dialed Mom's number. We hadn't talked now for more than ten days, and she didn't know what had happened to me or what I had been through. The last time we spoke I lied to her and told her I was perfectly fine. I was glad that I was still alive for her to hear my voice and be happy about it.

Usually, there was no reception because the government had control of all the carriers here and they had disabled the telephone networks most of the time to limit the communication in and out of the city. They obviously didn't want the rebels to communicate with each other, and they didn't want us to give the world outside any description of what was going on in here. But from time to time, they would allow phone calls to go through for a short period.

"Mom, hey it's me, how are you?"

Before she even spoke, I could hear happiness in her breath and a relief that I was still alive, and it didn't take long for tears to also find their way into the conversation as she said, "Zayn, my love, I'm so happy that you called. I have been praying for days now for this moment!"

"Mom, don't cry please. I'm okay, I swear, it's all good here."

"Son, you don't have to lie to me. I know that you are trapped in the devil's den so how could it be all be good for God's sake?"

"No, Mom! Believe me, we have food, and we're okay. I'm with Farah and Jasmine most of the time, and they are such great company. We are taking care of each other and hopefully we'll get to see you soon."

"I'm so happy you guys found each other. I can't imagine what would have happened to you if you were there alone. How are you, Zayn? Talk to me, please. Tell me what is happening there."

"Mom! I'm okay, I swear on my life I am. I've gotten used to being here and it's not that scary anymore. The people are sticking together, and we are hoping for a way out of this mess."

"Okay, Son, just take good care of yourself. I promise, Bassem and I tried everything to come and get you out of there. Don't you ever think that I gave up on you! I'm not going to stop trying, Son, I swear. Just have a bit more patience."

"Mom, it's okay, Uncle Jamal is also trying to find a way out of here for us. Hopefully, he will be successful."

"I can't hear you, Zayn!"

That was that. I realized they were about to cut the signal again.

"Mom, if you can hear me, just know that I love you and I'll talk to you soon, okay?"

And, it just went silent. I felt a little better after hearing Mom's voice. To be honest, even though I thought I had learned to live with the pain that missing her caused me, no matter how old I was, she treated me like a baby. And as much as I pretended that it bothered me, I actually felt safe and comfortable relying on her like one.

I went back in, and as soon as Jasmine saw me she jumped up and hugged me so hard to the point where I couldn't even breathe.

"Your majesty, I see you liked the books I brought you."

"Of course, I did. Even though they seem so big and

complicated. But Farah said that they were the first books she ever read and that I would enjoy them a lot, so thank you so much, my dear knight."

"At your service, my queen."

The three of us went to the kitchen and pretended that we had a variety of options to go through when it came to what to cook for dinner, but in reality, there was just canned soup, rice, and some flour to make bread with. But it was better than what we had been having for weeks now, so we were excited about tasting something new for a change.

We settled for the soup because it was the easiest thing to prepare and none of us could be bothered to go through the process of making the bread. We got the dining table ready and sat around it eating and laughing as if nothing was wrong in our world. I think the spirit that I had felt earlier today when I was at Uncle Jamal's place came with me and it affected us all. We moved to the couch after Jasmine insisted, because she was tired from all the energy she used while we were having dinner and wanted to lie down. So, she sat next to me, used my shoulder as a pillow, and started to fight the sleepiness she was feeling.

"Are you going to sleep, your majesty?"

"No, of course not. I need to take care of my kingdom and defend it from all its enemies." she said, with her eyes closed.

"You can do that in the morning, my queen, you need to have some rest now. Here, I'll carry you to your bed."

"No, Zayn, I want to stay with you guys. I'll sleep here, okay," and she jumped to the other couch. "Don't make any noise, you two, okay? Otherwise, I'm going to have to punish you for disturbing the queen's peaceful shuteye."

"You actually believe that, you little midget?" said Farah, laughing.

I covered her mouth and said, "Your orders are something we will never defy, sleep well, my queen."

It only took her a couple of minutes to actually fall asleep, and Farah pulled out one of Shakespeare's plays and we started diving into it page by page, one scene after another. The play was *Love's Labour's Lost,* and it was very Shakespearean! How did I know that? I didn't understand anything, and the poor, best soulmate to ever exist had to explain every page we read. The story was mainly about the King of Navarre and his search for answers through his studies together with his friends. It was interesting for Farah because she loved that kind of thing, and I took great pleasure watching her fall in love with a book and get passionate about the characters and the events that were taking place in the imaginary world the book created for us. It was very cold that night, and there was no electricity. The electricity hadn't been stable for the longest time. Sometimes we have it for a few hours a day, sometimes it was gone for a week, and we had to endure the freezing weather without any heat. We were both under two blankets and still we couldn't stop shivering because of how cold it was. Farah had the hand outside that she was holding the book with, and her other hand was between mine as I used my breath as a heat source, blowing it into her palms and making her feel warm. For once, the universe collided together and made this night a beautiful one to remember with how quiet it was outside. We enjoyed the silence for a change, and relished the wind's sighs that gave our place a romantic feel, together with the moonlight that was the only source of light we had.

From time to time, the clouds would stand between us and the light, turning our room into a dark paradise that we still felt safe in. We didn't need any light for us to feel each other's presence. Sometimes I would hold her hand tightly in mine and look at her smiling because she realized that even if we were a million kilometers away in the darkest, most obscure area on Earth we would still find one another just so she could complete me and I could do the same to her. After everything I had been through, I could finally throw what I used to believe in away and say that you don't need any help to find your soulmate! The fate that I believed in now would take you to each other, and then, and only then, your soul would light up as it had never done before. I wished that everyone could experience the feeling that was floating through my veins like the oxygen that she was to me. It's something that is way above love and all types of affection. It's a feeling of invincibility assured by the fact that nothing could tear us apart and no one could destroy what our souls had built.

It was around one in the morning, I was kind of sleeping, and Farah was next to me, still reading the book, when suddenly we heard a loud knock on the door.

Thirteen

I only remember me standing in front of the door and looking through the peephole, fear spreading into my body, paralyzing every millimeter of it. I froze there, and everything went silent for a moment, until a louder knock came to wake me up, sending me running towards Farah.

"People with guns! Try not to wake Jasmine and carry her upstairs. Don't make a sound, don't say a word, no matter what you hear. Lock the door and just stay there until I come and get you, okay?"

She gently grabbed her sister and ran with her upstairs. Looking at each other, we understood the circumstances we were in and knew that this might be where our story ended. God, if you have decided that this is the end, please let it be a merciful death for all of us, and if not, please don't make us go through an ounce of pain away from each other. They kept on knocking and it grew louder every time, so as fast as I could, I hid the books, threw away the covers, and walked to the door with my heart about to jump out of my chest.

"Took you long enough to open the door! We were just about to invite ourselves in," said one of the bearded animals that was at least three times my size. I counted, and there were at least eight of them. I stood there like a puppy facing hungry lions, not knowing what to do or say.

"Brother, is that anyway of talking to our friend here? Come on, he was just asleep, he wasn't going to let us wait outside in the cold. Isn't that true, my friend?"

"Yes, sir. I apologize, I was asleep."

"What, are we strangers? Invite us in!"

"I apologize, please come in."

They walked in as if they owned the place, and with dirty shoes and a disgusting smell they spread the scent of death and terror that escorted them wherever they chose to go. They all looked very similar, except the one who started talking to me. It looked as if he was the one calling all the shots, and I was assured of that as he sat on the couch, pulled out his gun, and looked at me.

"Come on, sit down with me. Don't be afraid! This gun will never be pointed at you, we don't hurt our own! Tell me, are you here alone?"

I sat facing him and said, "No, sir. I'm here with my two sisters. They are asleep upstairs, please don't hurt them, sir!"

"We aren't here to hurt anyone, Brother, your family is our family!"

"Zayn, my name is Zayn."

"We aren't here to hurt anyone, Zayn, we're here to help you, Brother, help you see the truth and a life worth living."

I stood there silent and terrified, looking at them, not knowing whether I should reply or just keep nodding and agreeing with everything he said.

"There is this horrific image that people have painted of us, and it looks as if everyone believes it, even our own brothers, like you. It's an image that describes us as savage animals with no mercy, unleashed hounds looking for blood, destroying everything in our way.

"And that image is absolutely correct, my brother. We are all of that and so much more, but only when we need to be. You have to remember that we are here fighting in the name of God, fulfilling his will, and laying down his rules. These people don't know what's best for them, they are lost in a well of sins, and we are here to show them the truth that they couldn't see for all these years. Do you agree with me, my brother?"

The venom that was crawling in my body every time this guy spoke crippled me, leaving me incapable of saying a word and all I could manage was to avoid making eye contact with him and keep nodding yes every time he asked me a question.

"I knew we would be on the same page. Didn't I tell you, Haidar, this guy won't cause any trouble," he said, looking at one of his dogs that was standing behind me.

"Now, Zayn, as you know, this evil world that we live in is trying to gang up on us and make everyone believe that we are a cancer that they need to cure. And their treatment is bombing everything that moves, killing our brothers and sisters everywhere. They are opposing the cause that we are fighting for, and that leaves them in a place where their life is no longer beneficial to the society we are trying to build, a society that will guarantee people like you a future that you deserve. But we will only be able to achieve that if we stand together. Strong, young men like you need to help us fulfill our purpose here, and fighting among your brothers is the highest prize you can ever get in your life. Carrying a gun and defending your land like the lion that you are is what we're hoping to see. Defeating the enemy and sending death towards them is the only response they will get from us as long as we have good men like you."

The words 'death' and 'fighting among your brothers' woke me up from the coma I was in. Was this guy asking me to join his mercenaries? The people who killed Omar's mother and thousands like her. People who terrorized us for months, and now he wanted me to be a part of them? I was so scared that if I said no he would show me his true colors and make me agree one way or another, but I had to at least try to avoid this mess.

"Sir, I don't think I'll be a good addition to your army. I mean, I can barely hold myself standing up, never mind carry weapons and go into battle! Also, sir, I'm taking care of my two sisters. If something happened to me they would have no one else here."

"I know that you have people who depend on you, and I want you to know that even though you would be fighting for the cause, you will have everything you wish for, my friend. There is plenty of food. It will be more than enough for all of you. And most importantly is security, and you will even have a family to build, a woman to marry, and children to raise along with everything you ever dreamed of. As for your sisters, they can serve a role in this as well. How old are they?"

"Twenty-two and eleven, sir."

"I give my word that they will be protected from any danger, and they will be safe as long as you are doing what you need to do. The twenty-two-year-old will get married to one of our high-ranking soldiers, and he will keep her safe and protect her from any harm. The younger girl is not that young anymore. She will also serve a role just like her sister, no worries."

With every word he spat, the happy world I had created with my Farah slowly started to diminish, and the plague that we escaped for a long time had finally got us right where we couldn't run any more. I wanted to scream and jump at him, killing him with my own two hands. I wanted to reach out for the gun he held and empty it in his brain, killing the devil that lived inside him, but unfortunately, I wasn't brave enough or stupid enough to do any of that. I just stood there is silence, thinking about the horrible image he had just put in my head. Someone marrying Farah? Blood on my hands, and Jasmine lost between this animal's hands? Really, God is this it? Is this your way of taking everything from me? I was lost, just lost.

"You see, Zayn, we are good, rational people, so I'm going to give you time to prepare yourself. Because I know it could be scary for you. It's a new world that you are being introduced to, but you need to know it's the world of righteousness so take your time. I'll be back here in six days, and I hope I find you and your family ready for your new test. Remember, you are doing this for God Almighty, not for me, and definitely not for you. But if you say no, it means that you are taking the other path and choosing sides with the devil, and honestly, I don't want to think about what will happen if you do that."

"Okay, sir, thank you."

They started leaving one after another, and he stood and put his hand on my shoulder. He gave me a look that will probably haunt me forever, a glance speaking louder than a billion words, a 'you don't have a choice' look, and confirmed the look with what he said right before I closed the door behind him, "Don't run, don't try to escape, there is nowhere we can't find you."

I locked the door behind them and turned around to

see Farah slowly coming down the stairs. She looked right through me, and with no words to say, she just held me so tight, trying to make me feel better. And for the first time, her magic touch wasn't capable of doing that. I was sure she heard the entire discussion and knew what they were offering and what the consequences were of saying no. I held on to her, feeling the warmth of her tears on my neck, and we stood weakened by the misery and pain life kept throwing at us.

"I can't imagine any one of them touching me, Zayn. I'd rather die than get married to one of those animals. And Jasmine, oh, God. I can't, I just can't picture what kind of a person she would grow up to be after this. I want to die. I really want to. Don't you think we have had enough of this world? I'm losing everything I ever cared about. There is no chance of me seeing my parents again, and I'm going to lose you, Zayn. Who will I be without you? I jus…"

"I wish I could say I have a way out of this. I wish I could save you and Jasmine from this. I wish I had wings just so I could fly you out of here. But it looks as if we were cursed from the beginning, Farah. Cursed to live with what we feel for each other in a world that is going to do all it can to stop us from existing, and prevent the love we have between us from growing like people our age would normally experience. Our days together are probably numbered now, but I have to say this, just in case we lose each other.

"You taught me how to live, Farah, you showed me how to breathe and you were the only happiness I ever knew. You will always be the one good thing that came out of all of this, and as sad as this is becoming, I would go through it all over again if it meant that I'd get to live this with you one more time.

"I know this feeling, or maybe I was introduced to its first chapter when my father died. That's when I first learned about pain and agony. Back then, I thought that was as sad as it gets in this chapter, but now I get to live with losing two of my loved ones, two stars that lit my world after years of darkness. I guess some people are meant to live in obscurity."

Farah completely lost it in my arms, and started to scream and cry, and trying to calm her down was like trying to tame fire with drops of water.

"What did I do to deserve this? What did I do to be here? Why am I being punished? This isn't fair, why was I even born here? I will kill myself and end my misery!" She ran to the kitchen and held a knife, pointing it at her heart.

"I will leave this hell and go and break God's door down. I'll ask him why he put me through this. What did I do to deserve being here? Are you happy now, God? You're even making them take the one good thing that kept me going this long!"

"Farah, please calm do…"

"You shut up, okay. You be quiet! You have nothing to live for anymore, they took everything and are even breaking us apart. I hate you. I hate not knowing you before. I hate not being able to live a normal life with you. I hate that every time you leave I start worrying that you won't come back. I hate that in seven days you are leaving me for good and you don't even have a choice. I hate you. I hate me for loving you this much. I love you and all I want now is to die with your love pumping in my veins. I just want this pain to end!"

I held her so tight that I thought she wouldn't be able to breathe for a moment. We both crumbled to the floor, holding each other as if we were inside a hurricane, fighting the wind to not blow us apart.

I took the knife from her hand and said, "Farah, we're not going to cave, we'll walk out of this city if we have to. If we die trying then let it be. I'd rather die next to you than live for a long time away from you. So please stop crying. We pinkie promised that we weren't letting go of each other, no matter what this life threw at us, remember? Don't worry, we are both going to keep that promise until our souls leave our bodies. And even if that happens, I'm sure they are going to keep on living together in another world, in another existence where they don't have to be afraid as we are."

Fourteen

After a long, stressful night, I woke up around 8 am to find myself sleeping on the floor with Farah lying next to me. I woke her up. We were both so exhausted from the tears and the scenarios we had played in our heads about how we could escape this. I begged her to go to sleep in her bed for a little longer. Meanwhile, I planned to go and see Uncle Jamal and talk to him about the crazy proposal I was given.

I noticed that there were an unusually large number of people in the street today, people talking to each other and kids running everywhere playing football as if there was nothing to worry about. Last night was the first night in weeks with no air strikes or attacks on the city, and I think that gave people hope that it might be over for a while, and things might change for the better. I didn't know if I should laugh or cry if they believed that. Maybe it was time to go back to being normal, but I didn't know if there was normal around here anymore. I was sure that the fiends that came to disturb the sad life I was living yesterday didn't only come for me. I was certain they would knock on every door in the city and break every dream and hope anyone had about getting out of here. I was sure there were many people thinking what I was thinking right now and looking for a way out just like I was. We were all doomed to be a part of something that we never signed up for. I hoped I didn't see the day when neighbors, brothers and friends would stand on opposite sides, pointing guns at each other and killing one another.

I could see Uncle Jamal in front of his house, sitting on his plastic chair, holding a cup of coffee, and enjoying the sun. As soon as he saw me walking towards him, he smiled and waved at me thinking this was just a normal day when Zayn came to visit. *If you only knew what was going on with me, Uncle, it would wipe that smile out for ever,* I thought. He stood, went inside, and left the door open for me. I followed him in and he was there in his living room, smiling, searching for something in a pile of papers he had on the table.

I said good morning to him, but he didn't reply. He just pointed at the couch where he wanted me to sit and wait for whatever he was looking for, so I did.

"How are you, Zayn? Is everything all right, you seem upset."

"I don't know where to start, Uncle. It looks as if I'm going to be one of them after all."

He laughed, and without even looking at me he spoke, "They came to recruit you, didn't they?"

I was so choked by the way he was talking about this. It looked as if Uncle Jamal had lost it, or he was on his way there. And his manners agitated me.

"Why are you laughing? Did I say something funny?"

"Oh, look who's angry now. Relax, Son, you don't have to be upset like this."

"Are you serious, Uncle? I think I made a mistake coming here, it seems like you're having fun and I don't want to bother you with my problems."

What in the blue blazes is wrong with him? Is what I kept saying to myself as I stood up and started walking towards the door.

"Oh, here it is." He shouted, "Zayn, bring your ass over here! I said, bring your ass over here! I thought you wanted a way out of this hellhole, so sit down."

"Wait, what?" What did he say, a way out? I sat down, and he kept on looking at the piece of paper he had in his hands, and said, "Zayn, do you know how to get to Cesar's Beach? The one on the other side of the city."

"I've never been there before but I think I can manage, why?"

"Well, it's a bit far especially as you have to get there on foot. It's around twenty kilometers and I w…"

"Uncle, please tell me, is this the guy who snuck your son out? Is this another one of his trips to Cyprus?"

"Why do you think I'm so happy? He's the one and he came to me last night and told me about this opportunity. This is the last trip he's going to make. He's not even coming back. They tried to recruit the youngest of his sons, so he said that there is no life for him here anymore. But he still wants payment for this."

"Money isn't a problem, Uncle. I'll give him whatever he asks for. I have some money put to one side for the dreams I was hoping to achieve."

"Oh, Son, it will be all right. When you breathe the scent of freedom away from here every dream and every hope that was killed because of this will be brought back to life. So, here is his number. I'm going to give you my satellite phone. It works everywhere, but you must keep it hidden. If anyone sees you with it you will be crucified and killed for it, and I mean that, Zayn. You have to be careful."

"I don't know what to say, Uncle. I'm so grateful. I'm forever in your debt. I'll never forget this; I swear on my life. You have no idea what you saved me from, Uncle."

I never thought I would get tears of joy one more time here. I was the definition of being high on the feeling of happiness. I kept on hugging the poor old man until he pushed me away for fear of me suffocating him. I was on my way out, but he called for me to sit down with him for a couple more minutes. He sat in front of me and started to bring wisdom to my ears as he always did, but I would always remember the last thing he said to me, "Zayn, this world we are in is going to ask a great deal of sacrifice from you for it to let you go free."

I left Uncle Jamal's house filled with happiness even though I was a little scared about the journey ahead. I kept on thinking about the trip all the way to the port at Cesar's Beach, and about the cold that we were going to have to deal with, and let's not forget the demons that were lurking everywhere for a chance to kill us for seeking a way out of here. But I knew it would be worth it, and that Farah would be over the moon with happiness and joy for the chance we finally have. I just needed to call the guy and ask where the payment was going to take place. I ran as fast as I could and couldn't remember ever wanting to scream from happiness as much as I did that day.

Farah was still asleep in her bed when I got back, so I stood there looking at her, wondering how happy she was going to be hearing the news. She looked so beautiful and calm, and I felt guilty for waking her up, but I honestly couldn't wait, so I got on my knees, tickled her nose, and whispered, "Farah, wake up." She opened her eyes and for once she wasn't angry with me for waking her up.

She just smiled and said, "You have no idea how much I'll miss waking up to your beautiful face, my soulmate."

"Farah, wake up, it's serious, please!"

"What's happened to us now?"

"I don't know, but I was thinking today and said to myself, 'What's the harm in joining these guys?' I mean, their offer was kind of decent last night, and I was thinking we should accept it. You would be married to one of them, but you would be safe. And you'll just have to learn to live with his beard scratching your face every time he kisses you. I don't think it's as bad as we thought it would be."

She kept staring at me bluntly, and I thought she was trying to process what I had just said. I never felt more scared in my entire life when she looked at me and said, "I'm sorry, did you go crazy or something? Are you serious? His beard? Oh, God, I want to puke."

"Farah, just think about it rationally and you will see that it's the best option we have."

"Leave, Zayn, leave my room please. I just can't look at you right now."

I looked at her and couldn't keep myself from laughing any more. She was so upset, and I knew it was stupid, but I teased her just so she would experience double the happiness later.

"Farah, pack whatever we need for a long, scary trip, we are getting out of here!"

"What does that mean? For the love of God, if you have something you want to say, please just say it!"

"Farah, my dear, I hope you like your hair getting wet

because you are going on a boat trip out of this hellhole. I found a way out. Well, to be more precise Uncle Jamal found an escape, and he gave me the mobile number of the guy who got his son and his family out. And I'm going to call him later and check where and when we need to be ready. The departure is from Cesar's Beach, which is twenty kilometers from here, and that is the scary trip we're going to have to take."

I held her hand and looked at her beautiful eyes, and as her cheeks turned red I said, "It looks as if this reality ain't so rough after all."

I could swear that every time she hugged me it felt like it was the first time she ever had, and if it wasn't stupid I would probably hold her in my arms and never let her go. As much as last night was sad and horrible, the news we got today changed everything in the house. Farah went to wake Jasmine up and tell her there was a chance for us to escape from this nightmare. I looked at her running in her pajamas to her sister's room, looking as cute as she always did, and I felt blessed with the feeling of happiness that was filling my heart. I didn't think there was a feeling better than the one that overwhelms you with joy when you see someone who means the world to you happy because of something you did.

Fifteen

I sat in the living room and dialed the guy's number, hoping it was going to be easy to reach a deal with him, and surprisingly enough it was. He was quite nice, especially because Uncle Jamal had already spoken to him about me. The money part was a little extravagant, but when I thought about it, we were literally buying our freedom, safety, and getting the life we had lost back. So, it was worth it even though he was strict when discussing it. He didn't want to go under four thousand dollars each, and it was a take it or leave it deal. So I took it and I'd leave the problem of finding the money for later. He said that we need to be at Cesar's Beach around 4 am, not a minute later because they weren't waiting for anyone. This was his final trip, so he was taking almost all his family members with him. He was insistent about the fact that we shouldn't be followed, and if we were caught we should never say what our intentions were or where we were heading to. We made a deal that we would meet tomorrow so I could pay him and discuss the final arrangements.

Happiness settled in the house that had witnessed so many good and bad memories that would live with us forever. Farah came down and I told her about my conversation with our fellow savior, and she was ecstatic about finally seeing that the universe had brought the light back in our direction. The only thing that we needed to find a solution to was the money and how we could pay the whole amount.

"Farah, I have around half the total amount needed, and we need to find a way to pay him the rest."

"My parents left us just enough to buy groceries and stuff like that, I don't have the rest, but do you think he would take my ring and my necklace together with a couple of rings that Jasmine has? They are twenty-four carat gold so that should cover the rest."

"I don't think he'll mind, after all it's still money. I'm going to discuss it with him tomorrow and I'll try to convince him that it's all we have. Don't worry, liberty is calling your name, my dear soulmate."

We spent the rest of the day high on happiness. Farah packed some clothes in her backpack, and Jasmine was jumping all over the place so excited that she was going to see her parents soon. We all knew there was a high risk that this adventure might end with us deep in the ocean, or maybe it could end with us being captured by the criminals that ruined our lives but we chose to ignore the risk for the moment and just enjoy the fact that we at least had a chance. It wouldn't matter if the sea decided to stand alongside the things that had destroyed us here and use its waves to end every hope we had of getting out alive. This was a one-way trip with one chance to get on board, exactly like Noah's Ark.

"Farah, he said there will be two boats ready to take people out of here." I said, while we were standing in front of her closet with her trying to decide what was the best thing to wear for the journey.

"That's great, because it means there will be a lot of people and it won't be that scary in the middle of the dark, vast ocean. Do you think this will look good on me?" she said, while she held a black wool shirt.

"Yeah, but it also means higher risk of us being discovered. And for the love of God, are you worried about how you will look on that boat?"

"Jeez, relax. I just want to go out this purgatory in style. What's the harm in that, Mister-I-Hate-To-Look-Good?"

I burst out laughing as I remembered how funny she could be at times.

"Oh, you're so funny. I'm going to miss you more than anything!"

"Miss me? Why are you going to miss me when you're going to be stuck with me for the rest of your life? The moment we leave all this behind, Zayn, it's going to be a fresh start. The start of a life that probably won't be perfect or amazing, because I don't know what I'm going to do or where I'm going to end up. But the one thing I'm certain of is that I want you there by my side. I want to have a relationship with you like normal soulmates would, not holding each other every day hoping that the roof of the house doesn't crumble on our heads at any second. You were my cornerstone through this rough time we experienced together, and I want you to be that forever. Didn't we pinkie promise on that a long time ago?"

I looked at her with a smile that probably spoke louder than all the words of affection in the dictionary.

"The deep blue shirt will look perfect on you. It's going to be freezing cold and the wool shirt isn't a clever idea. If it gets wet it's going to be very heavy and you won't be able to move as fast as you need to."

"See, Zayn, without you I'll make all the wrong decisions. You have to be with me like, forever and always."

"I will, dear, I'll never let you go. I'm going to check on Jasmine and see what she's doing and I'll make us some food, okay?"

"There's yesterday's rice. If you want it, you can have it if you're hungry. I'm too full of joy, I couldn't eat anything, I swear."

"You are so cute when you're happy. I'll be downstairs, take your time."

Jasmine, on the other hand, was twice as excited as Farah and I were. She was jumping all over the place, screaming and singing her favorite songs, pretending that she was talking to her parents, hugging them, and telling them how much she missed them. She was amazing, and I was probably happier about her getting out of here than me. All of this happiness came, and she still didn't know anything about the crows that landed with their death offers yesterday. I sat down with her, and she started to go on and on about how much her parents were going to love me for what I had done, how I was her best friend, and that she loved me more than anyone. The best part for me was that she wasn't scared of the sea or the fact that we were going to walk there in the middle of the night, not even knowing if we were going to make it or not. She was brave and seeing all of us this excited helped her not to fear the unknown we were walking into.

Sixteen

Nothing is worse than waking up to the sound of terror blowing up your eardrums. The quiet time we had yesterday was long forgotten when the angels of death came back for their usual visit, and it looked as if they were here to stay. The house was vibrating from the enormous amount of bombs that were being dropped randomly on the neighborhood. The three of us were looking at each other in silence, and I think we all shared the same prayer hoping that none of these bombs or burning barrels had our name written on it.

My meeting with our fellow savior was in half an hour, and for me to get there in time I had to leave in the middle of the firework fest that was taking place outside. We were scared but we also knew that we didn't have a choice. With tears and prayers, she begged me to take care of myself, and with a hug and a pinkie promise I vowed to her that nothing would stand between us and getting out of there.

"I swear, if you don't come back in one piece I'll never forgive you to the day I die," she whispered in my ear while holding me tight.

I couldn't help but stop in the middle of the road and yell at the top of my lungs, hoping that she would be able to hear me through all of the loud explosions, "Don't worry. As long as your voice is in my ears and your soul is mixed with mine I'll be okay. I'm invincible, remember?"

She was putting on an 'I'm worried' face, but that made her crack a smile. And with that beautiful image giving me strength, I started my journey in the middle of the storm of death that was tearing what was left of the city apart. I think I was the only person who left his nest that day. No one else was crazy enough to do so, and even the rebels were nowhere to be seen. The dust and smoke covered the city with a thick layer that stood between us and the sky above. I looked up and the only thing I saw was a continuity of a solid yellow and grayish color that kept getting darker and darker with every explosion I heard. I wasn't going to stop and let fear control me, but I was also hoping that the guy would be there and all of this wouldn't be for nothing. Every couple of minutes, the ground would shake underneath my feet and helicopters, or death toys as Jasmine called them, kept dropping bombs, some sort of flammable barrels, barrels containing acid, or a liquid that not only exploded but afterwards turned into a giant ball of flames that devoured and burnt everything in its way.

A couple more days like this and the city would be levelled to the ground and no one would be able to live there.

Through some miracle, I made it to the meeting point we agreed on and looked around the place, but no one was there. Doubt was getting into my head and I started to really get mad at the guy for not being a man of his word, especially as it was thirty minutes past our rendezvous time. The bastard insisted that no matter what happened I should be there on time, and if I didn't show up I'd miss my chance of getting on his boat. I tried to calm myself down, and since I had no other option to choose from, I sat in the middle of the road with a clear view of every entry that led in there, determined not to leave until the guy showed up and we made our deal.

Two hours passed, and I lost all sorts of hope that the guy would show up. Even the bombing slowed down, and the guy still didn't appear. What kind of an asshole was this man? In the past two days, I had experienced all sorts of feelings from sadness to fear, all the way to joy and happiness, and now, here came disappointment and failure to end our two-day-long story of hope. I got up, cursing the day that my mother gave birth to me and brought me into this world. I prayed that a bomb would fall on my head, freeing me from the sadness I was going to bring to Farah by telling her that it wasn't true, that we might as well cave to the reality in front of us.

I was about to leave there when I heard footsteps behind me and turned around to see two people with guns walking towards me. I looked and the terror that I always knew came to me in a different way this time. I started laughing so hard. I guessed my prayers had been answered and instead of a bomb ending my sadness two idiots were here to do the job.

"What are you doing here?" one of them shouted, as he pointed his gun at me.

"Just out for a walk, sir. Fresh air you know!"

I dodged the first punch, but the second one found its way onto my cheek, and I fell to the ground. Painful? Yes. But I was used to this. So, I just tried to get up. After all, this wasn't the first time this had happened, and I couldn't be bothered to defend myself to be honest. It would be over soon I kept saying to myself, until I heard someone yell at them, "Leave him alone. That's Jamal's friend, you idiots."

I looked around for the source of the voice and saw an old man running towards me, waving at them to stop bouncing their fists off my body.

"I apologize for being late, friend. We had to take care of some urgent business and it required more time than I thought. Are you okay?"

"Yes, I am, sir. Don't worry about it, please, it's just a misunderstanding apparently."

"These two are my sons, and they help me do business around here. You know how it is, you can't trust anyone these days, so please, apologies for what happened, they sometimes get carried away."

"It's okay, sir, let's talk business."

"Yes please. Jamal told me about you and I explained everything to him and what I'm able to provide. Did he tell you?"

"Yes, he did. I brought you the money. I just hope it's enough for you. Look, I have $3569 in cash and the rest..."

One of his sons interrupted me and bellowed, "What rest? You think this is a charity? The deal was clear, you either have the money or you don't, you either escape this hell or you don't, it's very simple, dummy."

"No, sir, please hear me out. I have the money, it's just not in cash. There are four rings in here and two bracelets, and I swear all of them are pure gold, without exception. You can have them verified. Here, take them, please, see for yourself. You can kill me if I'm lying, but I swear I'm not, please, sir."

I looked at Uncle Jamal's friend and said, "Please, sir, it's not just for me, it's for people I really care about, people who don't deserve to be here. They have no life in this hell here. You have to accept this, please."

He looked at me and I was sure some mercy fell into his heart when he saw me begging like that, especially after the ass whooping I got from his sons.

"The day after tomorrow, 4 am. Cesar's Beach. You wait there next to the red flag you will see stuck in the sand. 4 am we leave, not a second later. If you miss it, it's your loss and as I said on the phone when we spoke, if anyone catches you, deny knowing me and tell them you're there on your own. And they better believe you, because if they don't you'll be responsible for whatever they will do to us and for killing the hope we have for a better life out of here."

"Thank you so much, sir. I will be there, and I'm forever in your debt."

"Let's go," he said to his boys, and we started running in opposite directions, them to wherever they came from, and me to the happiest house in the city and into Farah's arms. I was laughing. I was running, bombs were exploding everywhere around me, and I was laughing, even with the black eyes one of them gave me, that's how happy I was.

"Farah!" I yelled at the top of my voice, "Jasmine! Where are you guys?"

I have never seen someone come down the stairs faster than they did. Farah holding a Barbie doll and a look of "tell me right now what is going on" on her face. I had an evil thought on my way here to trick them into thinking that I had failed in convincing the guy and that he said no, but honestly, I just couldn't.

"Nice doll, pretty girl!" I said, pointing at the toy that was in her hands.

"Zayn, talk. What happened? You were away for almost five hours. I kept on playing with this stupid doll trying not to think about the outcome of the meeting. Tell me what happened."

"Zayn, please, am I going to see my parents any time soon?" asked the little queen, looking at me with her glowing brown eyes.

So, I held both their hands and said, "I would strongly recommend you pack whatever is necessary for a two-day trip, because, my dear Jasmine, you are going to see your parents."

She jumped in my arms, hugging me hard. "I'm going to pack. I love you, Zayn. You are my best friend, I love you, I love you, I love you."

Every time I saw one of the two beautiful flowers happy, I felt an overwhelming feeling of pride. I felt so invigorated being the reason that made the people I loved happy, and that actually could cure all the sadness I felt inside. On the other hand, Farah was still looking at me with a beautiful smile on her face. So, I interrupted her before she commented on the black eyes I had, with a little kiss on her forehead and said, "My dear, our prayers have been answered. The day after tomorrow will mark the beginning of the future you deserve, where you can go back to following your dreams and hopes and to being the beautiful, happy angel that brought light into the life of desperate people like me. We need to be there at 4 am. As he said, the boats won't wait a second past that. We will leave three hours before, so we make it on time. It's not going to be easy, of course, but we'll make it, I promise you we will. And please ignore the black eyes, I thought I needed to get them, so I looked badass on the trip."

That night was so dreamy. The three of us sat on the couch, and the two souls who were with me started to picture the future that was waiting for them outside. Jasmine was so excited to go back to school and she put the biggest smile on my face by saying, "Zayn, you know that in my new school I'll have so many friends, but you will always be my best friend, and no one will ever come close to your position in my heart."

It was crazy what hope could do to people. There was a sparkle in their eyes that was capable of lighting up the entire world, and don't get me started on what Farah was planning for her future. Yesterday, just yesterday, the world closed down on us, and we both thought that we were at the end of the road and our lives will forever sink in the darkness that was forced upon us. But God, or whomever was listening to us beg for mercy, somehow found a way out for us. And with it came the light and hope again that showed each one of us our purpose again. The goals that beautiful soulmate of mine had were finishing her studies and getting her degree. There was a university in London that she always dreamt of going to, and it looked as if all of this had happened so she might be able to pursue that dream. She could have gone before, but she never got around to it, and it was one of those dreams that you just convince yourself is so far away and not even worth chasing.

The good thing about the two of them leaving for Europe was that they wouldn't be treated like immigrants. Uncle Jamal told me it was going to be very hard for people like us to be accepted there. After all, we were looked on as intruders and parasites who grew suddenly in a place where they didn't belong. But Farah and her sister weren't like me. Their parents had family in Italy who could take them in any time, and they wouldn't have to go through the process that people like me have to. But what was funny about it was every time Farah talked about her future and her plans she would include me in everything. She wouldn't say I, but she would say, "We need to go there. We need to sort that out. We would love it there."

And I kept saying to myself, "My dear, beautiful heart, it looks as if you forget that I'm a copying machine guy, and if I was stuck doing that here, what do you think I'd be capable of doing elsewhere?"

It was sad, but it was the truth, and I saw and heard it loud and clear. But Farah didn't want to think about it that way, so I just played along and tried not to take the smile off her face.

We had dinner and packed the few things that might be of use to us on the journey ahead. Each one of us had a backpack and started to put in what was necessary; bottles of water and a set of dry shirts in case we needed them. I made sure they weren't heavy and we were able to walk with the weight on our shoulders.

They were writing their last memories and enjoying the ultimate moments we had in the house that witnessed the struggle and the birth of the love story that lit our lives in its darkest days. We were really happy when it was just us, when we were holding hands and making each other laugh but it was heart-breaking whenever we peeked through a window or thought about what the future holds for us here. I was extremely tired from the running and excitement I went through that day, so with Farah's permission I was able to sleep in her beloved bed. As my head rested on her pillow, the exquisite scent of the perfume she always wore tickled my nose and had me thinking of all the good memories I had with her. I didn't care if I was in paradise or in the deepest parts of hell as long as she was with me, showing me the light, and providing me with the strength I needed to keep going. I never wanted to think about my life without her, even though there was the possibility that whether we failed or succeeded, we might be separated. The thought of that terrified me but my angel taught me to always try to focus on the full half of the cup. In her head, we had already made it. Jasmine, Farah, and I were already living a happy life in the future she drew delicately in her mind.

God, I loved her. I loved her so much and didn't think that I would ever be able to express to her how much. I loved her to the point that, when we slept in the same bed together, I focused on holding her tight and looking at her gracefully breathing and admired how beautiful she was, instead of turning it into a physical thing where we would just do what everyone would expect us to do. I didn't know how to explain it even to myself, but have you ever loved someone so much that that love would overshadow every physical lust and desire your body made you feel for that person? I mean, Farah was very attractive, and God gave her a body that she would tell you was full of flaws. But, I swear it was drawn with the most gorgeous beauty trails anyone could ever think of. But still, I just wanted to hold her tight and make her feel safe. I know I wasn't normal, but what was in the twisted world we were in? My train of thoughts was slowly silenced by my body asking me to stop everything and just fall asleep. It didn't take long for me to give in...

"Sorry, did I wake you?" Farah whispered, trying to sneak herself into my arms without waking me up.

"No, I was wondering in my sleep what I was missing, and now you are here, I have my answer."

"You are the sweetest soulmate, even when you are half asleep. You can go back and finish your dream as it was about me. I tried to sleep on the couch, but it wasn't comfortable and

Jasmine kicks in her sleep, so here was the only option left."

"I'm offended that you went looking for comfort in other places before you came here!"

"Look who is so charming in the middle of the night. If you joined the rebels you could kill people using that charm of yours, because no one would be able to fathom it out and live with all the sweetness and love that is you. So, it's good that you won't have to use guns and get blood on your hands!"

"It's all good then. I'll kill people using my charm and you marry one of them and we stay here, okay?"

I felt her elbow in my stomach and she pinched my arm hard, saying, "Don't you joke about that! It's scary just in my thoughts. God, I hate you, Zayn!"

I laughed, pulled her even closer to me, and said, "In two days you will be free of every scary thought like that. Let's pray together that we successfully make it out of here."

"I pray we will, Zayn, believe me I do. And do you know what I also pray for?"

"What?"

"It's that we make it together unharmed. I honestly wouldn't want to live if something happened, and we lost each other. I just want to be with you forever, Zayn."

"Even if something happened and we were separated, we would always be together. We are soulmates, and we pinkie promised on it, so it's all good."

"Okay, pinkie promise me again that nothing will ever come between us!"

"Nothing will, Farah! And just as our fingers lock like this, our souls will forever be together."

"I hope so. Come on, let's sleep. Goodnight, my prince."

"Goodnight, my princess."

Seventeen

Today was judgment day for us and there was a hint of excitement and fear in all our faces. We were sitting down eating breakfast, and silence was the only conversation we had. Well, if you call a piece of bread drizzled in olive oil breakfast, then yes, we were having breakfast. But that wasn't what was bothering us. All of us realized that in a couple of hours our quest would start and we had to succeed, no matter what happened. It was more emotional and harder for Farah and Jasmine than it was for me. It had probably hit them that they were leaving the house they grew up in, leaving all their memories behind. I think we knew that we would probably never come back here and even if we did, there was no chance that this place would still be standing here.

"It's completely normal to be nervous, my queen," I said, looking at Jasmine. "Tonight, we will be facing the biggest challenge of our lives, but together we'll be able to make it out of here. I promise, nothing bad will happen to us."

"I hope so, I'm really scared."

"Don't be, my love, please. If the queen becomes scared then all her citizens won't be able to keep going, so you need to be strong for us, okay, dear?"

She smiled and said, "You always find a way to make me laugh. That's why you're my best friend."

"That's my job as your best friend. I'm not doing anything special."

Farah was following our conversation with a smile on her face, but that couldn't hide the fact that it looked as if all of the stress was starting to get to her as well. I pulled her chair, with her sitting on it, until she was very close to me, put my head on her shoulder, and said, "I know you're nervous. I know you're scared, but I want you to be certain that God won't let us down. He will protect us and guide us out of here. After all, he can't leave one of his angels in danger anymore."

"I hope so, and if it wasn't for how adorable you are I probably would have died a long time ago."

"Remember, dear, you gave me purpose long before I gave you the feeling of security you were talking about."

"I gave her a little kiss on the cheek and with Jasmine calling for her kiss as well, I said, "I'm going to see Uncle Jamal one more time and tell him goodbye. I won't be gone long, okay?"

"Okay, but be careful!" Farah said, holding her pinkie finger towards me, and we adorably pinkie promised as I left the house, trying not to think about how stressed and afraid I was about what was waiting for us that night. I was trying to exude confidence into both of them, but I was far more terrified than they were. I kept thinking and playing bad scenarios in my head, and couldn't find a way out from most of them. And that was one of the reasons I was going to see Uncle Jamal. I knew he would probably use his words to boost my confidence and make me feel a lot better about the adventure ahead.

"Uncle Jamal, are you here?" The door was open, so I pushed it a little bit and said, "Uncle Jamal, it's me, Zayn, are you here?"

"Yes, Son, I'm in the kitchen. Come in."

I followed his voice to the kitchen only to find him there wearing an apron with his hands covered in blood. He was holding a knife and really concentrating on whatever he was cutting in the sink."

"Uncle, are you okay? What is that blood? What are you doing?"

He laughed and looked at me, "Come, help me out. I'm cutting the rabbits that one of my neighbors got for me. He caught four yesterday, so he was nice enough to give me two, and now, since you are here, one of them is for you. So come and hold this so I can finish skinning it!" I rolled up my sleeves and stood next to him, following his instructions as to how to hold the rabbit.

"I'm really sorry, Uncle. I feel so bad because you always give me the food that is meant to be yours, and we both know that you probably need it more than I do."

"Don't be silly, Son, I'm sure there will always be more. And if not, what kind of a man would I be if I were full and the people I cared about were hungry. You are one of the few people left here that I really care about, so giving you this actually brings more joy to my heart than you will ever know."

"You are amazing, Uncle. I can't even begin to describe how much you mean to me. You literally brought me back to life when I thought I was too far gone, and I came here to say goodbye since tonight is the big night."

"So, you made up your mind?" he said, looking at me.

"Yes I did, Uncle. If it was just me I would probably be

too scared to do anything like this, but I must take the risk for Farah and Jasmine. Knowing that they are going to be safe makes me the happiest man on earth, and we are at the point of no return now, so just wish me luck, please."

"I understand, Son. I hope you get what you want. I can see it in your eyes that even though you are terrified about the trip you will do everything in your power to save the people you care about. And that will give you strength. Don't worry, you'll be fine. You are far stronger than you think you are!"

"Am I? The scariest thing I can think of is what would happen if we got caught?"

"There's always the possibility of failure, Son, and that is a risk you need to take. You are already sacrificing so much here, but you must go into this hopeful that you will manage to get what you want. Here, take this, keep cleaning it like I did the first one. I want to give you something. I'll be right back."

He disappeared into the room next to the kitchen, only to come back a few minutes later holding a small box that he put on the table and asked me to wash my hands and open it.

"What kind of a surprise is this, Uncle?" I asked, and he just pointed at the box. So, I sat down and uncovered what was in it.

"You'll need that, Zayn. Take it but be careful with it."

"Really, Uncle, a gun! I've never held one before."

"It's very simple, you point it at whatever stands between you and your goal tonight, and you shoot. Make your bullets count and don't be scared if you miss, just keep shooting until your enemy hits the ground. The gun has a silencer as you can see, so don't be scared of being noticed.

"And please, Zayn, please, don't shoot yourself."

"Don't be silly, Uncle. Don't you need this for protection?"

"I thought I did, but I have nothing to be afraid of anymore. I don't need it, but you do, so take it and be careful. Don't let anyone see it, okay?"

"Thank you, Uncle. I owe you my life and don't know what to say. If I died for you it wouldn't be enough."

"You don't have to thank me, please stop it. I just want you to feel better because what you are about to go through is something scary for anyone. But I want you to know that it's okay to be scared. Because only then will you feel bravery you never felt before, and you will find the courage you didn't think you had."

I honestly didn't know how to thank the man. He literally gave me everything, and I couldn't be grateful enough for the circumstances that put us in each other's paths. He was one of the reasons I would always smile when I thought about the years I lived here, despite every horrible thing I went through. We finished cooking the rabbits, and when I say we, I mean he did everything. All I was doing was standing next to him and making comments on how delicious it smelled. He cooked it with rice and some vegetables. Meat was something I had forgotten the taste of. Luckily, my princesses and I would get one more chance to enjoy a healthy meal before we left. He put my share in a little plastic box and said, "Zayn, go and share this with Farah. You need to eat well and rest as much as you can before you leave tonight."

"I will, Uncle. Thank you so much for everything, even though 'thank you' doesn't even come close to describing how I feel about everything you have done since all of this started."

"Go, Son, it's almost 3 pm. You need to get ready, but

please, before you leave promise me that if we never see each other again you will always remember me! Please be certain that I'm proud to have known you and of being able to call you my son while I could. You are so much more than you think you are. There is greatness, love, and passion in your heart that could be enough to cure the world from all the pain and hatred that has poisoned it, remember that and don't ever underestimate yourself."

I gave him a hug and left his place with tears in my eyes. Who knew if I would see him again, but that wasn't what saddened me. He was here alone, and everyone around him chose a way out of the town except him. He could deny it, but I could see the hope in his eyes that someday he was going to wake up with all of this gone and he would just go back to his café and being normal, as he once was. We both knew that it was a dream far behind us now, but I hoped I was wrong, and his dreams would turn to reality one day.

****

"Farah, where are you? Jasmine, come and see what I got for us." I called out as I walked in the house. For some weird reason, Farah was cleaning the house, and Jasmine was sitting on the couch reading one of her books.

"Farah, what are you doing?"

"I don't know, I just wanted to stay busy and take my mind off what was going on. Why are you so excited?"

"Yes, Zayn, what did you get for us?" Jasmine asked.

"Sweetie, I have something that will revive you from all the stress you are feeling. Just follow me into the kitchen."

I went in and quickly set the table with three plates, next to each one was a fork, and I begged them to sit down with their eyes closed. For most people outside our little, gray world this would seem stupid. I was getting excited about rice and a piece of boiled rabbit, and believe me that wouldn't have made sense to me six months ago. But things change. For the past ten weeks, and maybe more, we had been living on bread and olive oil. Sometimes, we managed to get some canned soup that didn't even taste good enough to be dog food, but we had to eat it. This meal meant the world, especially in the situation that we were in. Their eyes were closed, so I filled their plates with the rice and minced meat, and as soon as the smell made its way to their noses, Jasmin screamed, "I'm opening my eyes! This smells so good."

"One second, dear, please don't." It smelled amazing and I was drooling like an idiot, but this was probably the last meal we were going to have together in this house, so it meant a lot to me. I had made it special by getting the napkins, cups of water, and the ketchup Farah absolutely loved and ate with almost everything.

I laughed and said, "Okay, are you ready? Open your eyes now."

A look of surprise was on both their faces, which I was pleased to see because it then turned into smiles and laughter as I had predicted it would. The dish wasn't that special, and if we were back in the day it wouldn't have tasted as delicious, but everything was different now. For me, their reaction made it more pleasant and far more satisfying having one final meal with them. You don't realize the importance of things in your life until you lose them. For us, the smallest things meant more then than anyone could imagine. I would have done anything for a slice of pizza, a hot bath, or even for the sound of the TV working. We just missed everything now life was so black and white, and moments like this were just a few lines of color that made it through from time to time. We were happy, but not from the hunger we had been feeling for days, but for the feeling of nostalgia the meal brought with it that painted one last memory for us to share in the house.

"Zayn, where did you get all this?" Farah asked, as she poured ketchup all over her plate.

"I'll tell you if you stop eating so much ketchup, dear, it's not good for you!"

"Grandpa, you know there are two things I can't live without in this world, you and ketchup, so please stop pressuring me to break up with it."

"You forgot your bed. Don't you love it, probably more than me?" Jasmine yelled at her, and the three of us burst out laughing from the fast comeback our little queen said. Just like that, we were turning the last pages of our life there with laughter, hope, and smiles. We finished, and I suggested that we got some rest before we started our journey. So, we got ourselves ready, and I checked everything twice. The bags had everything we needed in them. We had our clothes laid out, I had the phone with me, and it was looking good so far. I had the idea to call the guy to check with him one more time and regretted it as soon as he heard my voice and shouted at me, "Did your mom drop you on your head when you were a kid or something? Do you think this is a tourist trip we're going on, dummy? Just be there at four am, and I hope you miss it just so you know that our trip is non-refundable."

The three of us crawled into bed. I was hugging Jasmine, Farah was doing the same to me, and I think we melted into one person that night. I loved these two beautiful people, and I was so scared of what could happen to them tonight. I was terrified but I couldn't let it surface, not even to myself, so I tried to hide it by closing my eyes. I tried to hold still as much as I could, so I didn't disturb the peaceful couple of hours we had left. Jasmine looked so beautiful with her eyes closed, and Farah didn't move, so I assumed she fell asleep too. She had her arm around me like a neckless made out of beautiful flowers that carried the scent a happy life would smell like. There was something about this girl that to this day I couldn't seem to understand, she always smelled like the most beautiful perfume mixed with an angelic scent that took me on a ride to heaven. It had me looking at all the flowers that grew there, wondering how anyone could smell more fragrant. My lips found their way to her hand and with that, I heard a gentle whisper, "Zayn, are you awake?"

"Yes, love. I couldn't sleep to be honest. I just keep on thinking about tonight."

"Me neither. Let's go downstairs, I want to say goodbye to our house. I feel that I'll never see it again and it's actually breaking my heart."

"I'm afraid if I move Jasmine is going to wake up and she needs to rest before we leave."

"Are you kidding, Zayn? You should know by now that even if a bomb fell inside this room she wouldn't wake up. She is the heaviest sleeper I have ever known. Come on, follow me, she'll be all right."

I got up, and we held hands as we took a last goodbye tour of the house. Farah was really upset, and with every room we went in she would describe tons of memories she had with her family, and teardrops were goodbye notes that she would leave after closing each door. The war took everything from us and there was no words I could use to comfort her. I was just there for her, so she didn't feel alone. She held my arm tightly, trying to seek comfort in the one thing that she knew would never give up on her. We made it to the living room and sat on the couch. I got on my knees facing her, and she was very sad with tears running down her face.

"This broke my heart, Zayn. I love this place and it hit me earlier that I'm leaving all of this for good."

"I'm sorry. I would give my life a million times over if it meant things would go back to normal, but unfortunately, I can't."

"If they made you choose between living in all of this terror and fear and you still get to know me or having the security and safety we felt before all of this started, what would you choose?"

"Dear, oh dear, you don't know what you are to me, do you? I wasn't living before I knew you. I was just surviving. You are the air I breathe and the blood that circulates in my veins. Even if I died today I'd die with a smile on my face knowing that I was lucky enough to know someone like you, to feel your heartbeat against mine and play with your hair while you were gracefully asleep in my arms, to make you laugh and hold you close when you cried. I never believed in miracles or fate, but now I do. I know that someone up there wrote in the pages of my life that I'd be blessed at a certain time of darkness with a soulmate who could make me go through the deepest parts of hell with a smile on my face. Farah, it's you I'll always choose. I'd even choose you over myself."

My attempts failed at holding all of this in when a few tears made it to my eyes. I was really broken inside, and Farah's question got to me in a sense where I didn't want to live in a world without her. Ever since my father died, I had lived with one rule in my life, stating that no one will be in your world forever. And I accepted that as the only explanation I could find for the loneliness I was living in. I built a wall and used it as a shelter from the pain losing someone could cause, and I hate to admit it, but it worked for as long as I could remember. I never became attached to anyone, and I was fine with that until I met her. And no, my walls never came down, but she walked right through them. From day one, she taught me that it was okay to be attached, it was okay to be scared, and it was beautiful to feel your heartbeat just thinking about someone. I was broken and didn't know it until I felt her putting my pieces back together. She gave me the feeling of invincibility and strength that had kept me going so far. The world could come together and try to bring me down, and the universe could conspire on how to make me suffer, but with only her in my heart I was sure I could survive. I could feel her warm breath against my neck, and I was sure she felt my teardrops on her cheeks. It was a moment when our souls felt the need to remind us that it was the way we were meant to be; close, afraid, and in love.

I don't know how, but we started looking at each other's eyes, letting them say what we were too afraid to talk about. And with every blink, we got closer until I felt her lips press against mine. My senses were flooded with an overwhelming feeling of comfort words could never describe. It wasn't just a kiss; it was drops of devotion that my soul unknowingly craved for years. She held me so close until I was able to feel her heartbeat against mine and the only thought that I was capable of thinking right then was, *Thank God she was my first kiss, and pray to God she will be my last.*

Eighteen

The clouds covered the moonlight that night, and it was at once both good and bad for us. Darkness would be our friend if it provided shelter and cover along the way, but it was also scary, and who knew who and what could be hiding behind it.

Everything was ready for us to leave, and I sat down with Jasmine one last time, trying to boost her confidence, as she was the one I was most worried about. They gave the place one last goodbye look, and with a lot of fear and hope we closed the door behind us and started the journey to the holy beach of freedom.

Everything was really slow, and we wanted to be very careful since we had plenty of time, the departure was set for four am and now it was only midnight. I estimated from what Uncle Jamal told me that the trip should only take four hours, but the problem was the streets we had to take were either infested with the rebels or completely deserted to the point where you felt as if a monster could pop up from every corner.

Half an hour of walking made us feel a little more comfortable with the situation. We were carefully advancing to our destination despite the couple of explosions we heard from afar. It was scary every time it happened, as the earth shook underneath our feet, but I was relieved that the military decided to bomb the other side of the city and we were lucky to be traveling in the opposite direction.

It was really dark, and we couldn't talk out of fear of being noticed, so I kept holding both their hands tightly, and with prayers and the kisses I blew towards Jasmine, making her smile, we continued our walk of freedom. None of us had seen these streets since this nightmare started, and it was choking to see what used to be a neighborhood full of life turned into a deserted cemetery. I saw the building I used to work in, and now it was barely standing, looking like a pile of stones and lost memories. I could hear the copying machine sound in my ears and Janice's yelling was echoing deep inside my broken, scared heart, and that got me thinking about that poor woman. I wondered if she made it out of here and I wondered did she ever think about the people she used to torture and what happened to them? I wished I could see her one more time. I knew it wasn't logical wanting to see the devil again, but I wished I could tell her I understood. The things that I had seen and been through here had opened my eyes to a reality I didn't know existed. People build walls just so they can hide behind them and I was sure that she wasn't as cruel as we all thought she was. Who knew what kind of wars she was fighting on the inside? *I understand, Janice! And I hope you find the person who shows you the way through the nightmare.*

My mom, my dear mother, was the one I was really missing. We hadn't spoken for more than three weeks now, and I didn't know if she were alive or dead, and she didn't know anything about me either. I was sure that the feeling of sorrow was mutual. I tried to call her before with the satellite phone Uncle Jamal gave me, but the call never went through. My mother knew pain, probably as no one else did, and I knew that me disappearing like this could kill her, but what could I do? *Mom, I'm sorry, because once again I'm the source of your pain. Mom, I'm sorry for the times I was rude to you when you married Bassem and I didn't understand you. I'm sorry that I probably will never be the son you wanted me to be, and I apologize for pushing you away when I was looking for answers. Sorry, Mom, for the times when you were sick and I wasn't there to hold you, and please pardon me for causing your pure heart pain and for making you go through it alone because I know that you loved me more than I deserved. Mom, please know my heart misses you and that you will never leave my mind. Maybe this universe decided to put me through this just so I could feel an ounce of your agony through the years when you raised me alone, with the entire world to fight, praying that I turned out to be the son I never became.*

"Jasmine, we'll be there soon."

"I need to rest a little bit, Zayn, my feet hurt. We've been walking for an hour now," said Jasmine, pulling my hand to sit down with her on a broken tree branch.

"Baby, it's not safe, we need to go." Farah gently said to her, as she tried to calm her down, but it didn't look as if it was working. It only made her more upset, and she started to tear up.

"I can't move any longer, I swear. Look, I twisted my ankle when we crossed that pile of rocks, and it hurts so much now."

"Okay, baby, don't be upset, we still have time. Let's rest here a little. Let me see your leg." I became really scared seeing her ankle like that. It was swollen, and she must have been in so much pain. I couldn't believe how brave she was walking with it like that.

"I'm sorry, Zayn. Farah, please forgive me. I tried to forget about it and keep going but it hurts, and I couldn't bare the pain anymore."

"Don't apologize, my queen. It will be all right. We'll rest here for a couple of minutes and maybe you'll feel better."

The three of us sat on the branch, and Farah kept trying to comfort her. I looked around the place, only to realize that we were in the middle of what used to be a school, but now it was just piles of dirt above piles of rocks decorated with chalkboards and books torn apart everywhere. They stood there as testament to the bright future the kids were building.

Twenty minutes went by, and things started to look as I wished they never would. Jasmine was in so much pain and Farah and I didn't know what to do. She broke my heart when I saw her weep, apologizing for slowing us down. She was such a brave soul for an eleven-year-old, but her leg really gave up on her. She tried to walk, but all of her effort was worthless against the pain she was feeling. I only saw one way out of this, especially as we were losing precious time now, so I gave her a little kiss on the forehead and said, "Jasmine, I'm going to carry you, okay? You need to give your bag to Farah, hop on my back, and hold on tight."

"I'm sorry, Zayn, for being such a stupid idiot. I really tried my bes…"

"Stop it, Jasmine," I interrupted her, "What are you saying? This could happen to anyone of us, and I know if it did our beautiful little angel would have the strength to carry us to the end of the world. Now come on, let's get moving, we've lost precious time and can't afford to lose anymore."

She wasn't heavy at all, but I couldn't move that fast with her on my shoulders, and the fear of missing our appointment started to creep up on me. We only had two more hours to get there, and were farther away than we should have been at this point. Farah realized that, and we looked at each other. Her beautiful, dark eyes spoke to me and asked me very sadly, "Will we be able to make it?"

I didn't know and was scared as well but I nodded yes, trying to exude confidence into her heart. We walked and walked, and I kept ignoring my body calling repeatedly for a break. We were walking a very rustic road, full of rocks, sand, and tree branches, so it involved a lot of jumping and stepping over things, and the queen was on my shoulders making it harder for me. I kept saying to myself, *Hold on, Zayn. Hold on, failure will mean death, torture, and a miserable life under these clouds.*

I felt more confident when we came across a sign that said Cesar's Beach 5 km. With an hour and a half left, I thought we might be fine. It was just on the other side of the cliff.

"Zayn, get down! Get down, get down!" Farah suddenly hissed. We took shelter behind a tree by the side of the road, and I whispered, "What is it, Farah?"

She pointed at the street we were supposed to walk along and what I saw freaked the hell out of me. It looks as if it was the devil's den, or at least one of them. The terrorists were everywhere and there was no way we could walk there. A car was headed our way, so we sprinted into the forest that covered the cliff and hid behind the trees. It looked as if they had watch patrols that secured the perimeter. I didn't even know how we got this far without being noticed, and it looked as if we were trapped. We couldn't even go back.

"What are we going to do, Zayn. If we get caught that's it, I'm running and I'm not going to stop until they shoot me."

"Stop it, we won't get caught, pull yourself together. The beach is on the other side of this cliff that the street we were supposed to take circles. If the road isn't going to get us there, we need to look for an alternative way, and I think I have one but it's twice as hard."

"We don't have a choice. So, whatever it is we need to go with it."

"Instead of circling around the hill, we need to go right through it. It's going to be very dark because the big leafy trees cover the moonlight, but as you said, we don't have a choice. Jasmine, are you ready, Sweetie?"

She tapped on my back trying to tell me that she was, and I felt that fear had taken over her to the point where she couldn't speak anymore. I refused Farah's request to carry her, and we started our climb very slowly, praying that after all of this suffering we wouldn't be denied the dream that got us here. The problem with the path we were taking was we couldn't see anything in front of us. Uncle Jamal had made me very cautious after he said, "If you can't see the road up ahead or the stars above you, you could start going in circles and might be lost there for a long time."

I wished the old man were here. He would probably have a way out of the situation as if it were nothing. I wondered if we made it out of here how cool of a story this would be. I could sit my children down one day and tell them about the day their father traveled on foot for more than twenty kilometers, he ran from explosions, fought terrorists, and carried people on his back on the way there. And not just any people, who knows what Jasmine would be like then and if she was going to be in my life. I learned that people come into our lives for a reason, for a purpose, but no one was here to stay forever. It could be a day, a year, or a lifetime, but at a certain point the separation was inevitable, and I knew that every bone in my body would love to see my future painted with Farah's brushes giving it the most beautiful look even Picasso wouldn't be able to achieve. But who knew what would happen and I sadly prepared myself for that situation to take place. I cared about her more than I did about myself, but sometimes things don't go as you plan.

Nineteen

My back began to give up on me and it spread weakness and failure all the way down to my legs, and they started to buckle. I fell twice, and my knees were bleeding from the scratches I got. But, every time I got up as we had to keep going. Farah wasn't any better, she fell a couple of times as well, and her hands bled, and she had mud all over her silky hair. I was so tired and felt my vision starting to blur. I realized we needed to rest.

"Farah, we need to stop. I can't keep going. I can barely breathe."

"Nor can I. I can't feel my toes. I think I'm bleeding."

"Sit down, let me see. Jasmine, here, take some water, we are just going to breathe for a bit."

We sat next to each other underneath a tree and used its trunk for cover. I took Farah's shoes off, and she whimpered as I untied her shoelaces. My poor soulmate was in real pain. Her toes were swollen and some of them were bleeding.

"It's so darn dark in here I couldn't see where to put my feet, and I kept on stumbling on rocks and solid tree branches. I hate this."

"It will be all right, Sweetie. I have some bandages that I'm going to wrap your feet in. It's going to hurt, so please forgive me. I have to clean the scratches with water first."

She kept biting her lip, trying to endure the pain she was feeling, and I tried as gently as I could to pour water on her feet and wrap them in a clean bandage. It was the last bandage we had from when Omar treated me, and it was just as well that I brought it with me.

"Baby, I'm sorry, but it has to be tight like this." I said, trying not to focus on the pain I was causing her.

The moonlight sneaked its way through the tree branches. This time it fell right on her beautiful face, and I saw it covered with tears. It was beyond physical pain to see my one and only in such agony. Jasmine wasn't feeling well either and I was beyond tired and exhausted. I knew we were all breaking down, but there was no going back.

I grabbed both their hands and said, "Beyond this pain and suffering lies our freedom. I know it hurts and it's so much pain to handle, but we have to keep going. There's no other choice. Pain is temporary, and if we do successfully get out of here we'll have our whole life to rest and get over it. We just have to hold on to the hope. Farah, I'm going to put your socks and shoes back on. Jasmine, baby, you are going to jump on my back, hold on, and keep praying for us. Okay, are you guys ready?"

"But, Zayn, you're bleeding, look at your knees," said Farah in a very sad and worried tone.

"It's not a big deal. It's just a couple of scratches. We have to go."

I felt that even the weather wanted us to succeed. The past couple of days had been really cold and it was very windy, but today it was different. At least something was rooting for us to win this fight. Riding the waves two days ago would have been signing our death warrant, but today, with the weather we were blessed with, it was possible.

It was like a poker hand, with some luck we might win, and maybe with a lucky royal flush. So, I hoped it didn't change with the upcoming cards. I was tying Farah's shoelaces and Jasmine was putting the bottle of water back in my bag.

"Zayn, I keep on hearing noises from over there," said Jasmine, pointing at what I could only describe as darkness and beyond.

"It's probably birds, or some animal. Don't worry, Sweetie, we're moving right now. Come on, jump on my back and hold on tight."

We started to move again. The beach was north from here and that was my only clue. I had nothing to help find my path except the tiny compass Uncle Jamal gave me, so I kept following it, hoping that I'd lay my eyes on the water soon. I felt that we weren't climbing anymore, so we should be at the top of the hill and if it wasn't for the darkness and the trees we might have been able to see the water from here. *A couple more kilometers to go, Zayn, you come a long way for this so keep going.*

I slowed down a little and let Farah walk in front of me. It was silly but I wanted her to be the first one to see the sea. I needed her to be the first one to feel relief and joy from accomplishing our mission. I knew there was still a long way to what we wanted, but even if we got on the boat and for some reason it broke down and everyone who was on board drowned, it would still be a more merciful death that the one we were promised here.

"Everybody, stop right there."

I didn't believe my ears. And when Farah turned around

to see who said it I didn't think. I didn't process what we just heard, I just screamed at her, "Run!"

Our attempt at escaping the devil's howl behind us was a complete failure because after a couple of meters I heard a gun cocking, and the monster spoke again in a more terrifying voice, "I said, stop moving or I'll shoot."

Jasmine pressed her head against my back and used her hands to cover her ears, trying to escape the reality of what she just heard. But I knew there was no escaping this anymore. I turned around to see my dreams being shattered, and for the first time I saw what death looked like. It was dark, sad, scary, and carrying a gun, pointing it at me. With that picture being reflected in my eye and killing my soul, I read Farah's lips saying a prayer, "God, please get us out of this."

We got on our knees as the guy with the gun kept screaming at us, and I looked around for any others, but it looked as if he was probably on patrol or something and our luck made us cross paths with him.

"What are you doing here?" he said, walking towards us.

"Please, sir, don't hurt us. These are my sisters. Our house was destroyed in the bombing two days ago, and we are trying to seek refuge somewhere else."

"Seeking refuge up in this hill. Are you going to build a house in the trees and live there? Do you think I'm an idiot? Speak the truth, or by God I will cut your head off."

"Sir, I swear, we were just afraid and wanted to use the trees in here as cover from the choppers above. You know they will fire at anything that moves. Please, we are just passing by. If you let us go we will be grateful for that until the day we die."

A smirk followed by an evil laugh was obvious on his face as soon as I said, "Let us go!"

To be honest, I didn't believe that he would, but I had to try to talk to this man. Maybe there was still some mercy left in his heart. He might have been like me, forced into this, and maybe he would see that we meant no harm and he would be able to find a place of pity in his heart and let us go.

"Please, sir, consider me as your brother and these as your sisters. We mean no harm to anyone. We just want to go somewhere safe. If you let us go you will never see us again."

"Coward. My brother wouldn't be a coward like you, hiding in the woods, afraid of what God has destined upon us. He would be holding a gun, fighting this evil regime, and spreading the word of God. You are a coward, and if it was up to me I would end your life right here. Where were you when all of this started? Probably hiding somewhere, too afraid to fight for your right for freedom, and that is, in itself, punishable by death."

At this stage, I pretty much gave up all hope I had of living beyond the next couple of minutes, and I could see Farah on my right crying, but at the same time I remembered that she said she would rather die than have them catch her. So, before she did anything stupid, I held her hand, leaned in, and whispered, "Don't you dare do anything stupid!"

"Sir, look, my sister is hurting. She is so young, and our parents aren't here with us. We have no one. If I joined the army with you no one would be able to put food on the table for them if something happened to me. Maybe I'm a coward, but I'm being one so my family survives." He got on his knees and looked me dead in the eye.

"God doesn't forget his people. Your sisters don't belong to you anyway, they belong to God and have a higher purpose in our fight. If you had been brave enough to die for our cause we would take care of them, they would have the honor to be wives of great, brave soldiers unlike their brother."

"He lifted his filthy hand and used it to move Farah's hair that was covering her face. He looked at her with eyes filled with evil desires and hunger, as if he hadn't eaten for days and finally had a piece of meat served on a golden plate.

"She is pretty, even with a beauty spot on her cheek. I think our leaders would enjoy her, or maybe I should keep her for me."

Fire ignited in my heart seeing him touch her like that. I wanted to jump on him and eat his heart out like a hungry lion. She was so disgusted by him touching her, and he was enjoying it so much. Probably an animal like that never touched anyone that beautiful.

"Sir, please stop touching her."

"Oh, look at the brother being protective of his sister. You know that in our equation she is more important to us than you are. She will make whoever is going to choose her happy, and give him children and soldiers who will carry their father's strength. Get up. Come on, pretty girl, it's time to move."

He pulled her hand hard, and Jasmine jumped on him, trying to push him away. I tried to get up when he reached for his gun, and boom, everything stopped.

Twenty

Everything went into slow motion, and I could feel my heart about to jump out of my chest. Farah's screams filled the place as the man who was dragging her suddenly stopped moving and his body slammed her to the ground. He fell on her, and I could see her trying to get out from underneath him, but I couldn't help her. I froze and fell on my knees unable to fathom what I had just done.

Jasmine was barely able to step on her leg as she got close to her sister and pulled her arm as hard as she could, until Farah was free from the weight of the dead body that was on top of her. *Yes, Zayn, a dead body that you just killed. A man's life is what you just took.* I thought it wouldn't be this scary to get one of these animals. When Uncle Jamal gave me the gun, I said to myself that if I had to use it I wished it would be on one of these bastards just so it silenced the anger that I felt towards them.

"Zayn, look at me. Zayn, please look at me!"

Farah held my head in her arms and tried to snap me out of it, but I wasn't there anymore. I wondered how they made it seem so easy. How people like him killed almost every day and then moved on with their life, as if it were nothing. I shot the man who was trying to hurt the most important person in my life, and I felt so guilty for doing it. He was twisted, and the devil had taken control of his soul and his body, but did I have the right to end his life? I was certain he had dreams, friends, and maybe family. And I took him from all of that.

I felt Farah's hand on my cheek, slapping me hard, not knowing what to do

"Zayn, please, my love, answer me. Are you okay? Talk to me please."

"I killed a man, Farah. I took his life. He is dead because of me."

"That man right there was going to end our dream and kill every ounce of hope we lived for these past months. I was going to be served to their leader, Zayn. Think about what you just did, what you saved me from. You breathed life into me so many times before ,but this is way more than that. Think about what they would have done to me, Zayn. Me, your soulmate, your best friend. I was going to get passed from one to another, as if I were a piece of meat that everyone could take a bite from. I know you feel bad, and what you did is making you feel sick, but just know that you, my love, you saved me."

I couldn't find words to describe to her what I felt. I knew that I had saved the three of us from a lot of pain, but I never wanted blood on my hands.

I took comfort in the only place I felt safe, in her arms. And I could see Jasmine sitting next to us, and tears pouring out of her eyes as she kept looking at the dead man lying on the ground. I felt Farah's pain through the rate her heart was beating and from how tight she held me, and I knew it wasn't because of the fear we were feeling. No, we both realized that the one thing we kept protecting her from was right there in front of her. The pure soul she had was now tainted, and she now knew the darkness that was probably going to chase her forever.

"We need to move," I said. "We need to move right now before someone comes looking for him. We need to be at the beach in thirty minutes."

I got up and put all my grief aside because I knew there was still time to fix this. At least all of this wouldn't be for nothing, so I went and carried Jasmine, and Farah got her bag. I don't know where the strength came from, but we started running. The fear we felt fueled our bodies with energy strong enough to make us forget our physical pain. I could barely see in front of me as the trees were so close and the leaves formed a wall that we kept powering through, and then suddenly, there it was. I could see it and I could hear its waves calling to us.

We took a moment to look around, and Jasmine pointed at the red flag that was standing on the beach representing the point where we should regroup. With fifteen minutes left, we needed to move quickly, and had to start the rough way down off the cliff. It wasn't that hard, or maybe it was, I don't even know. I remember falling three times with Jasmine on my back and I got up as if it were nothing, and Farah was stepping on all sorts of rocks, not caring about the pain she was feeling. It was as if we were high on drugs or something, and all our senses went numb except the one that kept screaming for the freedom the flag represented.

We got down and crouched underneath a tree a couple of meters from the flag. It was too risky to stay without cover next to it, so we hid there, waiting for a sign or someone to come pick us up. Farah gently leaned on me, and with relief and joy she said, "We made it. We still have a long way until we reach our destination, but we made it, Zayn, and it's all thanks to you."

"I did nothing except keep my promises, my soulmate. Here, I want you to take this gun and keep it hidden. Use it to protect yourself and your sister from any danger. Who knows what will happen, and I need to know that you will be safe if we are separated. But, remember to throw it in the water before the police in Cyprus go through your things."

"I don't need a gun if you are with me, Zayn. We won't be separated."

"No, please take it. For me. I need to know you'll be safe, no matter what. I'll put the safety back on. Look, you pull this back, point, and shoot. Don't hesitate, okay?"

"Fine, give it to me, but I won't need it. We'll be fine, I promise."

We rested for a couple of minutes under that tree, and I looked at my watch. It was exactly 3:56 am and I kept looking around at the water for a sign that we need to follow. I gave Farah the satellite phone and checked Jasmine's ankle. For some weird reason the swelling had diminished, and it looked better. She even told me that she couldn't feel any pain anymore. As they say, it's always darkest before dawn and I thought we might be around the dawn.

I felt a hand on my shoulder, followed by a man's voice, "What are you guys doing here?"

I turned around, thinking it might be another crow lurking around this place looking for dead, beaten-up meat like us that it could feast on. But things kept getting better and better. The man behind the voice this time was Omar, our neighbor, the doctor I owed my life to. He was apparently on a journey similar to ours, and Farah whispered at him while pushing him, "You scared the living hell out of me, Omar. Why did you sneak up on us?"

"What did you want me to do, yell hello, how are you, Farah, from a kilometer away and get us all killed?"

I laughed at his answer and felt happier knowing there would be familiar faces on the trip with us.

"After they killed my mother, I thought about every way possible to avenge her death. I wanted them to feel my pain. But then I realized that even if I killed ten or twenty of the monsters, as long as I was living here I would never be able to get rid of the pain they carved into my heart. So, I thought about a new beginning and letting their punishment be in the hands of the god they claim to follow, thus my presence here."

"It's good to have a familiar face with us. When did they tell you, you needed to be here?" asked Farah.

"Karim said be here at four am, not a second after."

"That's good, it's what they said to us. I hope they will be here soon."

It was 4 am, and there was no sign of them. I started to question the honesty of this Salem guy, and Farah tried to use the satellite phone to call him, but obviously it wasn't going through, and we started to get increasingly worried as time flew by.

Omar, on the other hand, wasn't bothered at all and spoke very highly of Salem and the business he was running. According to him, this Salem guy was working with the military, and he knows the area and how to hide very well. That's what makes him successful. He concluded that they were probably taking extra caution and making sure that they got there as safely as possible. But neither one of us knew what to wait for or where they were coming from. I took Omar to the side because I wanted to thank him for what he did to me before, and tell him how he saved me from dying when he helped Farah take care of me.

"Omar, I can't thank you enough for what you did and until my last breath on this earth, I'll still be grateful for that, but I need one more favor."

"Sure, Zayn, you and Farah are like family to me, whatever you need."

" I just want you to promise me that you will treat them like they are family if something happens along the way. They are stronger than you think, but I need to know that I can trust someone to finish this fight if I wasn't there to witness its end."

"I promise I will. I give you my word, so please don't worry."

I begged him a bit more and didn't stop talking until I was sure than he knew the whole story and I felt he was ready to take the risk for them.

Farah came closer to where we were sitting, held my hand tightly, and whispered, "We are like this, Zayn." And she pointed at our hands locked together.

"We will never be apart, and I know we are doing this, so we can get our lives back together and maybe build a future of our own. Look at me, Zayn! My life is wherever you are, and my future isn't worth living if you aren't a part of it."

I was lost in her eyes as she spoke, and the only response I found was to kiss her hand. The moon must have realized what she meant to me and what I wanted to say and suddenly got brighter, sending beautiful rays of light to reflect on her charming face. It lit it up one more time for me to see, for me to try to fathom how I made this beautiful creation find its way into my heart. I didn't think she had ever looked more beautiful, from her hair that fell gracefully on her shoulders all the way to her eyes that saw right through me, all the way to her lips that spoke melodies that my heart loved to hear, to her tiny nose that she used to tickle my neck every time she hugged me, jumping to her beauty spot that made her unique to me and to everyone who would ever cross paths with her. I wished I could be...

"Zayn, look! Look, there's a light flickering towards us." Jasmine shouted at me, and we all got up to see a boat that wasn't that far in the sea and it kept flashing its light towards the place where the red flag was pinned.

"Omar, do you think that is it, and they are calling for us?"

"It's risky, who knows, it might be the rebels playing tricks with us. Stay low, I'm going to check it myself. If it's all good the light will flicker three times, then it will go off. Only then can you consider it safe to come, okay?"

"Okay, Omar," said Farah. "Just be careful."

He started to slowly run towards the boat and disappeared into the waves that separated us from the ride of happiness. I was so excited, watching the two angels next to me smile and the tears and sadness we had were covered with the overwhelming joy and sense of accomplishment we felt.

"It was worth it," I whispered to Farah.

She had the most gorgeous smile on her face as she said, "If I had to go through it all again just to be here with you, I would."

The light went off and our hearts stopped beating. I

counted the seconds, and then, one flicker, two flickers, three, and I said, "Let's go, let's go."

We lunged into the biggest run of our lives. I was holding both their hands thinking I'd be helping them keep up, only to find them pulling me so I could catch up. Even Jasmine who was hurt didn't feel the pain anymore. And that was the beauty of finally getting hold of something you really wanted, it camouflaged every pain you had to go through along the way and the suffering we felt made this happiness taste so much better. It pumped our hearts back to life. We had to swim to get to the boat, so I picked Jasmine up and we stepped into the freezing cold water and slowly came closer, trying to forget the cold that was taking over our bodies. I could barely feel my legs, and Farah's lips turned a very dark blue. The only thing that kept us going was the adrenaline that was going through our bodies. As we got closer, I could see Omar on the side of the boat, holding his hand out to help us get in, and as soon as I was within his reach, he grabbed Jasmine and pulled her in. I was even more relieved when I saw him putting a safety vest on her as well as covering her with a foil thermal blanket.

"One more person to go!" shouted the guy on the boat.

Farah was trying to say something, but there was no time for me to listen. I grabbed her by the waist, and with Omar's help she made it onto the boat. As soon as they got her on board, they started the engine, and the boat slowly started to move. I couldn't see much because of all the water that went into my eyes, but I could hear Farah screaming at the top of her lungs.

"Zayn is still down there, he is still down there, he needs to get in, please don't move!"

I lifted my head to see Omar trying to keep her from jumping off the boat, and I was scared that either she would jump, and they would leave her and go on with their trip, or because she was holding everybody down they would just throw her off. So, I got what little strength I had left, swam closer to the boat, and held on to the ropes surrounding it. She tried to pull me up with all her strength.

"Farah, stop! Please, you have to go, I'll be on the other boat, don't worry we'll be right behind you!

"What boat? I don't see anything here!" She turned to Omar and screamed, "Is there another boat coming? Answer me. Answer me, for the love of God!"

I couldn't see what everyone looked like, but I felt through their silence how sad seeing her like that made them. There was no way she was going to let them move, and in such situations they didn't take things like this very easily. I saw fear in Omar's eyes, worried that something bad might happen to her and Jasmine as he begged me to make her shut up.

"Farah, look at me, please look at me." I pulled her arm until we were just centimeters away. Her screaming stopped when our eyes fell onto each other, and I said, "Farah, you are on the boat, and you are a couple of hours away from seeing you parents. Think about Jasmine, think about the life we are going to have. I'll be fine, I promise you that. Please, you need to stop screaming. The boat needs to move. I love you and I always will. Here, give me your hand. Pinkie promise me that you will be safe, and no matter where life takes you it will always lead you back to me. Move." I yelled at Salem and Farah's tears were the last thing that I tasted as I kissed her cheek goodbye. And with that, the boat started to float away. Our pinkies held on to each other until the waves threw me back and it broke them apart.

They slowly started to vanish into the dark ocean ahead, and I kept on listening to the sound of the engine until it faded away. I turned around to see that I was surrounded by a dark infinity of nothing from all sides and I got scared. There were a lot of people around me, and then suddenly I found myself alone, and the cold made my feet and hands go numb and I found it very hard to breathe. So, I swam back to the shore and crumbled as soon as I touched the sand. I couldn't move a muscle, and my body kept on shaking, either from the cold it felt or from the pain it endured.

I started to cry because I realized what I just lost. I knew that this would happen eventually, but I never knew that it would hurt this much. There never was a second boat, and I knew that all along. There were only two spots, one for her and another one for Jasmine. Even the money we had wasn't enough for the three of us to get out of here. I couldn't tell them any of this, so I came up with the second boat lie and I didn't regret it and I never will. The only thing that I felt sad about was the lonely life I was going back to. Farah left and she took with her every fiber of my soul together with my heart that she had ruled ever since I knew her. I hoped she would forgive me, and I would pray that she would make it safely to wherever she desired.

You see, every one of us keeps looking for the answers to our lives and some of us continue the chase until their last day on Earth and they will leave without one. But I was lucky, I found mine, and for the brief period I got to live the most beautiful dream ever. And I lived it with my eyes wide open, focusing on the mesmerizing parts of it. I cry now because I lived all my life alone and I'm afraid that it will be like that forever now. Even if I make it out of here alive, which I seriously doubt, I won't be able to live without my heart. Even if I can go back to my mom and see her lovely face again, I won't feel complete because what is missing is something that can't be replaced by anyone.

Inside all this sadness a smile found its way onto my face when I remembered that she had one more thing from me that would make her smile. When she was asleep in my arms two days ago, I snuck away from her, grabbed a pen and paper, and I wrote her something. I wrapped it in plastic, but didn't know when the right time would be to give it to her. When I saw Omar I felt such a relief because I knew that he would be my messenger. I wrote her a letter, even though there weren't enough words in any language that could describe to her how much she meant to me, but I tried. And I remember every word of it – it's as if I wrote it on paper yet at the same time it was carved on my soul.

Dear Farah

By the time you read this I hope you have already made it safely to the other side of the world. You have no idea how hurt I am for making you go through it alone, but, Farah, believe me it was the only way. From the beginning I knew there were only two spots left on the boat and I chose you and Jasmine, and if I had another chance to make that decision nothing would change.

I know you are mad at me, and I can't write anything that will make you feel better, but this is completely and utterly my decision. Even though you have control over every fiber of my being this was up to me, so don't ever blame yourself for this. I'm writing this looking at you gracefully asleep in your beloved bed. The bed that witnessed everything we went through from the scares in the middle of the night, to the safe place I found in your arms as we slept, all the way to you taking care of me when I was hurt.

I'm looking at you and I never missed you as much as I do now, knowing that these might be the last memories we write together. The first time I ever saw you, I felt something different the moment my eyes were graced with the beautiful sight of you. That angelic face of yours was the gateway to the heaven I was in for the days we spent together. Even though you were in a hurry that day and probably thought you were a mess, believe me, you never looked more beautiful. You were wearing a black jacket and your flower printed pants, and that was the day you knocked on the door to my heart.

The fate I never believed in played me and with a little bit of luck we met again. So, I simply let you in, knowing that the life I hated and all the problems that were breaking my soul were just doing their job of leading me to you just so you could put me back together.

Farah, even if we never see each other, or even if you never hear my voice again, I want you to know that you will never leave my heart and it will never beat for anyone as much as it did for you. You are to me what the sun is to this world. The days we spent together are the fire that my soul needs to keep going, and even if God chose for me to leave this world today, or fifty years from now, I would never be afraid and I will stand before him with only one request, 'Let me see her, God! No heaven or paradise will be as good as seeing her beautiful smile.'

Farah, when this happens, I want to see you happy. I want to see you being the successful, beautiful woman I always dreamt you would be. And for that to happen, you need to let go. No, not forget me, but just let me go Don't live on the hope that one day I'll be back, and we can live the dream that we thought we would. I know that I will forever live among the blood cells that travel your body and that your heart will always have me in it, but sometimes that is the only way out. It will be hard, I know, but we are lucky, believe me. What we felt for each other and the moments that we spent together are far more than most humans get in a lifetime. And one day you will sit your children down telling them our story.

Tell them that once upon a time there was a boy who loved a girl so much that the word love doesn't describe what he felt for her. She was his miracle, his blessing, and his safe haven. He never felt happiness as much as he did looking at her smiles and hearing her laughs echoed across his heart until his last day on this earth. He was blind and God chose her to be the light that traveled through his eyes all the way to the lonely heart he had, painting for him the picture that he will always look at this world with. A picture of him standing alone surrounded by destruction, holding a smile on his face, a smile that shows that good things might be born out of the saddest circumstances we humans face. A picture of happiness that he didn't have an eternity to enjoy, but what he had was enough for him to leave this world feeling that he was lucky enough to experience how it is for his heart to love, live, and die for what he called the pinkie promise of a lifetime.

I love you, Farah, more than anyone will love you…
Goodbye.

I Pinkie Promise